# PRISONERS OF WAR

# THE SIMMERING INFERNO

## BRIAN CRAWFORD

EPIC
Press

# The Simmering Inferno
### Prisoners of War: Book #3

Written by Brian Crawford

Copyright © 2017 by Abdo Consulting Group, Inc.

Published by EPIC Press™
PO Box 398166
Minneapolis, MN 55439

Cover design by Christina Doffing
Images for cover art obtained from iStockPhoto.com
Edited by Gil Conrad

LIBRARY OF CONGRESS CATALOGING-IN-PUBLICATION DATA

Names: Crawford, Brian, author.
Title: The simmering inferno / by Brian Crawford.
Description: Minneapolis, MN : EPIC Press, [2017] | Series: Prisoners of war ; book #3
Summary: Józef joins an underground movement smuggling weapons and
kerosene into the Jewish ghetto in central Poland. When Germans march in, the resistance
strikes, but the Germans capture Józef making him lose more than just his freedom.
Identifiers: LCCN 2016931780 | ISBN 9781680763539 (lib. bdg.) |
ISBN 9781680763393 (ebook)
Subjects: LCSH: Prisoners—Fiction. | Prisoner-of-war camps—Fiction. | Escaped prisoners—
Fiction. | Interpersonal relationships—Fiction. | Survival—Fiction. | Human behavior—
Fiction. | Young adult fiction.
Classification: DDC [Fic]—dc23
LC record available at http://lccn.loc.gov/2016931780

EPICPRESS.COM

*Dedicated to all those who resist persecution and tyranny, in whatever form.*

*"Leave all hope, you who enter here."*
—Dante Alighieri

This story was inspired by real events of the Warsaw Ghetto Uprising, which occurred from April to May, 1943. The ghetto depicted in this novel, however, is fictional, as are all characters.

*February 1945*

KOMMANDANT STRAUSS PACED IN FRONT OF THE prisoners assembled in the *Appellplatz*. The sun had not yet risen, but the Germans had forced the prisoners of KL Himmelweg out of their bunks at four a.m. for roll call—a little earlier than usual.

Near the middle of the rear column, Józef Maizner tried to stand at attention without wavering. Since Russ had helped him out of the quarry several weeks before, he'd regained much of his strength. But he was still weak. And he always felt dizzy just after getting up. It would take another hour for the blood to return to his frozen and stiff joints. By then, hopefully Éric would have reached his objective and the revolt begun.

From the southeast corner of the camp, the acrid reek of a smoldering fire lingered over the *Appellplatz*. The prisoners had finished extinguishing the fire, but hidden embers continued to spit fumes into the air. Even before the blaze had completely faded, the Nazis had conducted their search for any missing weapons.

In the corner of his eye, Józef watched Julia. Like a tree in the breeze, her body wavered, clearly on its last leg. Józef's heart clinched. Beyond just getting through the wire, he wanted to help her out. Protect her. Ever since he'd been arrested in the ghetto, ever since he'd arrived in KL Himmelweg and met Julia in her wounded and weakened state, he'd felt protective of her. Not that he loved her, but he cared for her. And he felt a duty.

One that he'd failed at in the ghetto . . .

# TWO

*April 1943*

JÓZEF MAIZNER TUCKED HIS CHIN DOWN AND THRUST HIS HANDS INTO his pockets. He tried to pull his head below his scarf and overcoat collar, but through the bitter cold, the screams still stung his ears. Screams, cries, dogs barking, whips cracking, and Germans shouting—he'd heard it all before. Since he'd come to the ghetto a year before, this had become a regular occurrence—the third time in two weeks. But it didn't make it any easier to hear.

A transport was leaving from the *Umschlagplatz.*

*Umschlagplatz*—the "transfer square," as the Germans called it. Right in the middle of the ghetto and across the street from the synagogue. Where the Krauts rounded Jews up to be "transferred." *To where?* There were rumors, of course. Some said they were going to labor camps in the East. Some said Madagascar. Some said they were going to be murdered in the Ukraine. But as much as Józef hated the Germans, he never believed they could be slaughtering so many people. How could they? Not only was it impossible, but if they were doing it, Russia would know about it, and they'd put a stop to it. After all, the Ukraine was in Russian territory.

*No,* he reasoned, *it's just another transfer.*

Józef walked from his apartment and north along Bulwar Chopin. A hundred meters ahead, a black-and-white, rail-crossing gate was lowered in front of the tracks crossing the ghetto from west to east. Two German guards stood on either side of the street, their rifles slung over their shoulders, while two others paced in front of the closed barrier. Each held a submachine gun. Józef knew that just to the right of the crossing, obscured by the four-story block of flats that filled the length of the city block, there was a large platform where hundreds of Jews were standing right now. He knew there would be families clutching each other, some with suitcases, some without. And that the crowd would be surrounded by German officers with whips, snarling dogs, and Mausers. He knew there was probably a train steaming there now, just out of sight, with anywhere from ten to twenty cattle cars, their doors open and awaiting the hundreds of deportees who were being herded into their gaping mouths.

He knew all of this because he'd once seen the whole scene from the synagogue.

"Halt!" One of the pacing guards stopped in the middle of the street and faced Józef, just as he was crossing Wenceslas Street. "Halt!" he shouted again, pointing his gun towards Józef. "No Jews near the *Umschlagplatz* during a transfer!" The soldier pointed to his right. "You must make a detour! Mieszko Boulevard that way! No exceptions!"

Józef nodded and turned left onto Wenceslas

Street. He walked down the street and the screams and shouting faded behind the blocks of dilapidated buildings. Now, his path took him to Mieszko Boulevard, which ran north-south and parallel to the wall separating the ghetto from the rest of town—the Aryan side. Józef lifted his eyes and looked straight ahead. Like a massive wave of red and brown, the brick wall loomed upwards, cresting in rolls and rolls of barbed wire. On top of the bricks, the Germans had shattered bottles and placed the razor-sharp shards into the cement before it had dried. The result was a wall that would shred anyone trying to cross into the city—that is, if he were foolish enough to try and escape this way.

Every fifty meters, the wall's monotony was broken by a six-meter high watchtower. During the day, two guards peered out of their perch and into the ghetto, their machine guns gazing back and forth like dragons ready to spit fire on the poor souls below. One of the men held the weapon's grips, while the other supported the weight of the chain of bullets protruding from its side. At night, all that could be seen from the towers were the massive, glowing Cyclops eyes, which spit beams of white into the darkened ghetto, ready to catch anyone breaking curfew. Every now and then, machine gun fire would echo through the night, letting the ghetto's inhabitants know that the eye had seen someone out of their home. Maybe the person had been visiting a friend or family member. Maybe the person had been surprised by curfew and was trying to get home. Maybe the person was trying to escape . . . Whatever the reason, the result was always the same: a wide-eyed, bloodied body lying in the street the following morning.

Where the Germans would let it rot as a warning to everyone else.

Józef walked, and moans wafted up to him from the buildings, where there were always hundreds of people lying or sitting, asking him for help. "Please, *fraynd*," they'd mumble in Yiddish, "friend, please. Some water. Some bread. Please . . . " Every now and then a body lay in a heap, often well into decomposition. The Germans often let bodies rot where they fell, as a warning. Before death, disease, and starving had become so common, Józef used to stop and help those still clinging to life. Even if he didn't have any food or water to give, he would lift people out of the *dreck* and help them sit on a stoop or stair. At least this gave them some more dignity than lying on the ground in the filth and rat shit. Now, the year had hardened him, and he tried not to look at every person that lined the streets. He'd almost become blind to the bodies that were little more than skeletons, their yellowing skin pulled tight against their bones. He hardly noticed the overpowering stench of urine and diarrhea, as well as the squeaking and rustling of monstrous rats scurrying up to the dying to nibble on toes or legs . . .

When Józef arrived three blocks north of the *Umschlagplatz*, he turned right and headed towards 24 Stanislaw Moniuszko Street, a large, imposing building that served as the Town Hall before the war. The building was three stories tall and painted yellow, though the paint was now peeling, revealing the grey plaster and stucco underneath. Unlike most of the buildings in the ghetto, the Town Hall was not connected to the neighboring buildings. It stood alone, and was surrounded by patches of brown and dying grass. In the center of the façade, a bare flagpole was thrust into a brass holder above the main double doors. Before the Germans had arrived, the red-and-white Polish flag had hung there. Since the creation of the ghetto, however, the Polish flag had been replaced with the red, black, and white Nazi flag.

But each time the Germans put it up it would disappear within a day.

Józef climbed the six steps to the entrance and opened the door, which was always unlocked. "Reduces suspicions that way," Rabbi Gerschner had said. "If the door stays closed, you want to know what's behind it. But if it's open . . . " Once inside, Józef walked upstairs, past the brown and dusty walls that once displayed the portraits of Poland's heroes from past wars. Now the only portrait remaining was that of Adolf Hitler, that Satan incarnate, who strutted like some Czar or Roman Emperor, a red-and-black speckled cape draped over his shoulders while he gazed into the future of his Thousand-Year Reich.

József spat in front of the Führer.

---

"*Gutn morgn*, good morning," József said, opening the door to Room 123 and stepping in.

The other members of the *Judenrat*, the Jewish Council, were already there and seated around the rectangular meeting table. They were Feliks Zielisky, a fifty-four-year-old former civil servant and current Council leader; Oskar Starek, a forty-seven-year-old former professor of languages at the Warsaw University and current liaison to the Nazis; Aron Miazga, forty, a former farmer; and Hermann Metzger, fifty, a German Jew and baker from Munich. They stood to greet József, who, at twenty-one, was their youngest member. This had always made József chuckle, because here he was, just out of teacher-training school, meeting with four other men in their forties and fifties, to discuss the organization and administration of the ghetto.

"You are valuable," Feliks had told him when he'd been invited to join three months before. "In your role as teacher you can help us to maintain the children's education, forbidden though this may be. Meeting with them in secret, of course, so the Nazis will never find out. Who knows? Maybe the *Judenrat* will need you for other things in the future? You have shown great courage in defying the Nazis by supporting our children. You have risked capture. Death. Time will tell."

Józef nodded at the Council members and sat at the table. He folded his hands in front of him and caught his breath from climbing the stairs.

"Thank you for coming," Feliks began. "You are healthy?"

"I am alive, hm," Józef answered. "And as long as I am alive, anything is possible."

"Yes, yes!" Aron chuckled. "As long as we are all alive! But that is not true for everyone, I'm afraid."

"Unfortunately, no," Józef sighed and looked out the window. He could no longer hear any sounds from the *Umschlagplatz*.

"How is your fiancée? Ana?" Oskar asked, lifting his eyes.

Józef looked down at his hands, which he wrung together. "Not well, I'm afraid. Thank you for asking."

"Is she still in bed?"

Józef nodded. "Each time I see her she's weaker, hm. I'm going to Grunwolski later," he lifted his head and stood up straight. "I've been told he's a great doctor."

"Yes, yes," Oskar agreed. "A great doctor, indeed."

"So," Józef looked around at the men, hoping to shift the subject from Ana. "There's a transfer happening today? I didn't know. Otherwise I would have come a different way."

Feliks and Oskar looked at each other.

"Yes," Feliks began. "The third in two weeks. There are great worries about what the Germans are planning. This is why we wanted to see you."

"Planning?" Józef asked.

"The ghetto has been here for three years," Oskar said, "and in all that time there have not been transfers like this. Before, the *Umschlagplatz* was where new Jews arrived into the ghetto, not where they left. The Germans have been asking me for lists of people to transfer."

"Lists? What lists?" Józef looked up.

"As member of the *Judenrat* I am obligated to comply. In Warsaw, a Council member refused, and he was hanged. So I comply. I try to choose men with no families, but this is not always possible. You understand."

"Where are they sent?"

There was a silence in the room. The men shuffled in place.

"No one is sure. But there are rumors," Feliks said.

"The rumors are growing," Aron added.

"Look," Oskar interrupted, sitting up. "We've been watching you. Beyond your work in meeting and planning with us. When the Nazis built the ghetto, they outlawed schools here. On pain of death, we imagine. But for the past year you have been here, you've shown courage in continuing to meet with the students. You've risked your life. You've proven yourself."

Józef studied Oskar, his head cocked.

"Thank you," he said. "Proven myself for what?"

The Council members looked at each other. Feliks cleared his throat, plunged his hand into his pocket, and pulled out a slip of paper that he slid across the table to Józef.

"We want you to meet someone," Feliks said. "His name is written there. And his address. He knows the situation better than we. And he can explain how you might help. More actively than we can, in any case."

"What do you mean, 'more actively'?" Józef asked.

"Well, the Germans may have their plans," Feliks tightened his jaw and glared at Józef. "But so do we."

# THREE

WHEN JÓZEF RETURNED TO HIS GARRET APARTMENT, HE bustled against the cold. Because his room was on the fourth floor and just below the slanted roof, the frigid winter air seeped in through the non-insulated slats above, it crept in through the cracked window and warped frame on the wall. And it rose upward from the floor. When he was at home, he tried to keep some coal smoldering in the woodburning stove. Between this, his own body heat and the meager warmth provided by five or six candles placed around the room, he kept hypothermia at bay.

Józef's room was three meters by four, and

anyone coming in had to duck to avoid hitting his head on the roof. The stove sat just to the right of the door. A few feet into the room, a small dining table with one chair sat pushed up against a lone window with one cracked pane. It looked down on Piotr Gamrat Boulevard below. Because the room was part of the attic, the window was just larger than a dinner plate.

Pushed up against the opposite wall, Józef's bed sat stacked with books during the day. At night he would place these on the table so that he could sleep. A small water closet with a toilet and a sink was opposite the dining table. During the warmer months Józef washed from a white, metal washbasin that he filled with the brown tap water. In winter he would go without washing to avoid the freezing water. When he was here, he drank only tea boiled on the stove. He was too afraid of cholera, dysentery, or God knows what else might be pumped up through the building's aging pipes.

Closing the door behind him, Józef stepped

across to his bed and knelt. He thrust his right hand under his mattress and withdrew a folding pocketknife that he opened with a click. Without hesitating, he grabbed his pillow with his left hand and plunged the knife in with his right, placing the point just at the stitching, so that it would be easier to repair the pillow later. Pulling the blade sideways, he opened a ten-inch gash with a dull ripping sound, revealing the yellowing stuffing inside. He closed the knife, placed it on the wooden floor, and worked his hand into the hole. He wormed his fingers in all directions, like some giant spider, pushing the stuffing to the side, plunging deeper, exploring every square centimeter of the pillow's insides.

His hand brushed up against something cold and metallic—that was it. He closed his fist around the object. He eased his arm out, stood, and opened his hand.

There in the middle of his palm lay a thick, golden ring. An embossed, leafy vine worked its way around the band, ending in an angular coat of arms on the top. Józef turned the ring in his hands, admiring how it reflected the dim, grey afternoon light trickling in from the window. When he'd come to the ghetto a year earlier, the Nazis had confiscated all valuables—watches, jewelry, ivory, gold. Before he'd been deported from his home city, he'd sewn the ring into the tail of his coat. The Germans had never thought to look. Now, this was the only object he owned worth more than fifty Zlotys on the outside. Since the Germans allowed the Jews to use only Ghettomarks, Józef had no idea what the ring might be worth.

"Papa," he muttered, gazing at the ring, "when you gave me this, you said it would be for my own children some day, hm. Maybe you will be right, but in a different way!" With a deep breath, he pocketed the ring and walked out of his garret, closing the door behind him.

Moische Grunwolski lived on the same side of the ghetto as Józef—to the south of the train tracks but just beyond Wenceslas Street. To get there, Józef had to walk by the *Umschlagplatz*, which had fallen silent since the morning's chaos. Józef hurried with his head down and hands plunged deep into his pockets. His right hand clutched the ring, which had begun to warm in his sweaty palm.

Józef crossed the square and glanced to his right, where the train platform lay opposite the synagogue—a building that had been there for three hundred years. When the Germans formed the ghetto, they installed the train tracks so incoming Jews would disembark directly in front of the holy building. Perhaps so that people would feel hope. No one knew. All they knew was that the Germans could not be trusted. Especially now that Jews were beginning to leave from the same place.

Józef stopped and looked down. There, in the middle of the grey cobblestones of the *Umschagplatz*, a tattered teddy bear lay face down, its rear in the air. Józef bent over and picked it up. A large black boot print marred the animal's belly. Józef looked up and scanned the square. The Germans had gone. Aside from himself, there was no one—not even any of the sick or dying that littered the other streets in the ghetto. A cold wind blew in, biting him in the face. He had the feeling someone was watching him. But he saw no one. At least no one outside. He tossed the bear back to the ground and hurried to the doctor's office.

"Yes?" Grunwolski cracked his door open and looked out. His eyes peered out from behind a massive black beard and bushy eyebrows. To the right of his door, a verdigris-covered plaque read:

MOISCHE GRUNWOLSKI
GENERAL MEDICINE

"Doctor Grunwolski?" Józef removed his hat and bowed. "My name is . . . "

"Józef Waleczność. I know who you are. You teach at the *shul*. Or rather, what pitiful excuse for a *shul* that we can manage. I have seen you about.

Feliks has told me about you. Says you have balls of steel."

"Yes, well . . . " Józef hugged himself and pulled his hands to his mouth to warm them. "May I come in?"

Grunwolski stepped back and pulled his door open. Józef stepped in and looked around. He was in a small, square room with four chairs pushed up against the walls. A waiting room. Since he'd arrived in the ghetto, Józef had never had to visit the doctor. He was one of the lucky ones.

"Please," Grunwolski held out his hand and led Józef through a door into his office. Once inside, the doctor closed the door and took a seat behind a wide desk covered with papers. Papers that seemed to have been tossed onto the desk in a hurry. To the left, a human skeleton hung suspended from a metal frame. Its left arm had been broken off and was lying on the floor. Józef sat in a cushioned chair opposite the doctor.

"What can I do for you?" Grunwolski asked,

sitting. He stared across at Józef as if expecting Józef to attack him. He folded his arms and breathed noisily.

"It's like this," Józef squirmed in his seat. "I need treatment. Not for me, hm. For my fiancée. At home. Her name is Ana."

"I see. What is her ailment?"

"I'm not sure. She's been in the ghetto for two years. I came just last year, and when I arrived she was already bedridden. We grew up in the same town, you see. Now she and her mother are all alone, hm. The last time a doctor saw her was months ago. Because they no longer have any money."

"Was it Doctor Stornak?"

"I don't know the doctor's name."

"It must've been. Aside from me he was the only doctor in the ghetto."

"Should I go to him, do you think? Maybe he would have a better knowledge of Ana's condition?"

"You can't."

Józef cocked his head.

"Why not? Is he too expensive?"

"No. He's gone. Transferred a month ago in one of those transports. I don't even know if he's alive."

Silence.

"I understand, hm. So do you think you could help? Perhaps come look at her."

Grunwolski sat back and crossed his arms.

"You know what I must ask," he said.

Józef put his hand in his pocket.

"I think so, yes."

"Do you have money? I'm not interested in these Ghettomarks the Germans are spreading around like some game or toy for us to play with. Or paper for us to wipe our ass. Times are hard. I'm afraid human compassion only goes so far these days."

"I have this," Józef pulled out the ring and slid it across the desk. Grunwolski's eyebrows raised and his eyes widened. He lifted the ring and drew it close to his face. He pulled his glasses down over his nose and stared at the ring, turning it over and over in his fingers.

"This is gold," Grunwolski said as a statement. Not a question.

"Yes. It was my father's. He died ten years ago."

Grunwolski looked up.

"This girl must mean a lot to you."

Józef was silent. He stared at the doctor and narrowed his eyes.

"Yes, hm, she—"

There was a knock at the door. Both men jerked their heads up. Józef placed his hand on the arm of the chair and turned around. Grunwolski stood and pocketed the ring.

"A patient?" Józef asked. Grunwolski shook his head.

"Maybe. I don't know." He glanced at the wall clock and turned back to Józef. "Let's see. Stay here."

Grunwolski brushed off the front of his shirt. He crossed into the waiting room and opened the front door. Józef kept his eyes forward, scanning the doctor's aging yellow wallpaper. Oblong diamonds crisscrossed a fading paisley, and several diplomas hung at odd angles from one another.

Józef started as scuffling and thumping from the waiting room tumbled into Grunwolski's office. The doctor was shoved in by the arms amid grunts and snorts. Józef stood and turned. Three German soldiers armed with submachine guns and pistols led Grunwolski in and pushed him forward, so that he and Józef stood shoulder to shoulder. One of the Germans wore a black leather trench coat, while the other two wore olive-green field uniforms.

Józef and Grunwolski now faced the doctor's empty chair. When he came to a stop, Grunwolski glanced at Józef and seemed to say something with only his dark eyes and bushy eyebrows. Józef had been in the ghetto long enough to know when to talk and when to keep quiet. Now was a time to keep quiet.

"*Hände hoch!*" one of the Germans shouted,

walking around the desk and pointing his Mauser at Józef. Józef raised his hands and one of the soldiers patted him down. The German reached his hand into Józef's vest and pulled out his identity papers. He handed the papers to the officer, who lowered his gun and flipped through the pages.

"Why are you here, Józef Maizner?" he asked, looking up.

"My back's been hurting," he answered, glancing over to the doctor. Grunwolski did not take his eyes off the German. "I needed Doctor Grunwolski to look at it."

"Your back?" the German answered, handing Józef's ID back to him. Józef nodded and lowered his right hand, taking his ID card. He placed it back in his vest pocket.

"Well," the German continued, "I am afraid that now is not the time for your exam. You will have to come back." He looked at one of the soldiers and nodded. The soldier stepped forward and placed his hand on Józef's arm. "We need to speak with the doctor here, about an official matter about which only he can connect the dots."

"*Komm*," the soldier pulled on Józef's arm. Józef looked back and forth between the soldier and Grunwolski, who narrowed his eyes as if to say, *Go ahead. I'll be alright.*

"*Jetzt mit mir kommen!*" the soldier spat, his voice becoming enraged.

With one last glance at the doctor, Józef backed out of the office and through the door to the street. His heart pounded. He shot a glance to Grunwolski's pocket. Grunwolski nodded again with his eyes before shifting his gaze to the door. Józef understood: he had to go, and he had to go now.

FOUR

JÓZEF LEFT THE OFFICE, HIS THOUGHTS SWIRLING. WHY had the Germans come? Was there any connection between the soldiers he had seen earlier and these three? Since he'd been in the ghetto, the Germans had more or less avoided the Jews, their homes, and their offices, unless they were arresting someone or meeting with the Jewish Council. But now? And the transports? As much as he wanted to linger behind and listen to what was happening in Grunwolski's office, Józef knew well enough to avoid the Germans.

Józef quickened his steps against the cold. When he reached Nicolaus Copernicus Street, a block away, he unfolded the slip of paper that Feliks had given him.

*Kazik K., 42 Mikolaj Street, fourth floor*

He saw from the address that the place was next to his school. Kazik's apartment probably looked out over the courtyard where Józef's students had played over the past two years. He wondered how much Kazik knew about him. Would he recognize him?

When Józef arrived at the building, the ground floor door was open. *Strange.* Normally the door would be closed and he would have to ring the bell to be let in. He stepped up onto the grey concrete steps and looked up and down the street. Aside from two children huddled together against the building's wall about seven meters away, no one was around. From several blocks away, some shouting echoed across the street walls and broke the silence of the early afternoon. The shouting ended as fast as it started, though, like a phonograph being yanked from a player. Józef couldn't tell what was being said, nor what language was being shouted—German? Yiddish? He didn't think it was German, because German had always sounded harsher to his ears.

"Hello?" Józef stuck his head into the darkened doorway and looked around. The building smelled of dust and mold. As if it had been closed for weeks, with no windows or doors allowing air in. A long, high hallway stretched straight ahead to the back of the building. Every fifteen feet or so, a door punctuated the smooth, grey walls. An aging wooden staircase rose from the warped, dark brown floor planks and stretched to the upper floors, winding around in an oblong rectangle. Looking up, Józef could see the yellowing bannister swirling in upon itself like a spiral.

Amid creaks and squeaks of wood against rusty nails, Józef climbed the stairs. On the fourth floor, Józef saw four doors. Each was closed. He glanced back at the slip of paper, pocketed it, and stepped up to Room 19. He knocked on the door and waited.

*KNOCK. KNOCKKNOCK. KNOCK. KNOCK-KNOCKKNOCK. KNOCK.*

There was a pause, followed by scuffling and slow footsteps from inside the apartment. A click of the doorknob, then another, and the door swung open. A cold breeze swept up the stairway and into the door, chilling Józef's back and neck.

"Józef?" The man framed in the door was short and gaunt. His hair, which before the war had likely been thick and flowing, was shorn close to the scalp, revealing a constellation of red bumps and scabs. His stubble was long and crooked, as if he had been trying to shave with a pair of scissors and a trembling hand. Józef scanned his memory but could not remember ever having seen him.

"Yes, I'm Józef, hm," he answered, holding out his hand.

"Kazik. Pleasure." The two shook hands. "Come in. Please."

Józef stepped in. Kazik closed and latched the door behind him. Józef looked around. The apartment was much larger than his own garret. A small hallway led down to a larger living area. There were two doors on the right and one on the left. All three were closed. The ceiling was checkered with panels just larger than a man's shoulders.

The two walked into the living area, which was furnished with a brown and dusty sofa, a coffee table stained with pale rings from glass bottoms, and an armchair with torn and sagging upholstery. In the corner, a black wood-burning stove simmered and radiated some warmth. A few feet away from the stove, there was a rickety table. A samovar sat in the middle of the table.

"Please," Kazik motioned for Józef to sit in the armchair, while Kazik plopped down on the sofa.

"So you teach?"

Józef nodded.

"Yes. I've been seeing the children since I arrived. We meet in a different spot each week. I used to teach in my hometown. Sioło."

"Sioło?" Kazik's eyes widened. "That's where I am from! When did you get here?"

"A year ago this past September."

"I'll be damned! We were perhaps on the same transport. Were you on the train that stopped for a day just outside of Lublin?"

"Yes, that was it!" Józef squinted. He tried to remember ever seeing Kazik. "Where did you work?"

"Outside the city. My family farmed. Cows and chickens. But we were called up. The Germans hated us even more because we were Communists as well as Jews."

"Did you know Max Schmeichler? Wasn't he active in the Party before thirty-nine?"

"Yes, of course. A great man. The Krauts killed him just before I was called up. I sometimes wonder if they didn't find my name on some list along with his. But I don't think so."

"Do you have any family here?" Józef asked.

Kazik grew silent. "No," he said. "My mama and papa hid in a neighbor's barn when we got the call-up. Some friends and I were able to hide them under some hay with air holes, food, and water. That was two years ago. I have no idea if they're alive now."

"I'm sorry," Józef said. "All we can do is hope, hm."

"What about you?"

Józef shook his head. "My parents were killed when the Germans came to Sioło. Not because they were Jewish, but because they were Poles. The Germans were trying to send a message, I imagine. Even though my parents weren't involved in resistance. So here, it's just me. And my fiancée, whom I hope to marry. Once we get out. And she gets better."

"Where is she?"

"She lives on Chopin Boulevard with her mother."

"What sickness does she have?"

"I don't know. Nor does she, hm. She's been

getting weaker for over a year. I just went to the doctor."

"Doctor Stornak? But he's—"

"Deported? I know. No, I went to Grunwolski."

"A good man. A *mensch*."

The two sized each other up. Józef sat up straight. His hands were large and his shoulders and arms still muscular, despite the food restrictions. He was lucky to count himself among those who had not yet gotten sick from dysentery, cholera, typhus, or any of the other diseases that inflamed the ghetto. Kazik had not been so lucky. He was recovering from cholera, and the violent diarrhea had cost him forty pounds. Before the war, he was not one to be crossed. Large and imposing, he had once looked like someone capable of pulling a tree up with his hands.

But no longer.

"So," Kazik broke the silence. "Feliks has spoken highly of you. Says you are one of *us*."

"Us?"

"Let me show you."

Kazik stood and stepped up onto the sofa, which creaked under his weight. He stretched upward and placed his hands on the ceiling. With a tap and a push, he lifted one of the ceiling panels and slid it aside, sending a trickle of white plaster dust down onto the dark brown sofa. He looked back at Józef, who eyed his moves carefully.

"You'll need to grip the beams that support the ceiling, here and here," he said, smacking his hands down on two large, thick planks running perpendicular to the wall. "If you grab onto the tiles themselves, you'll pull the whole thing down. Hmpf!" With a grunt, he pulled himself off the sofa and into the darkness of the attic. He rose and the muscles and sinews in his arms bulged and tugged. Hoisting his upper body through the hole, he rotated and sat on one of the planks, before pulling his feet up into the darkness.

"Come on!" Kazik snapped, sticking his hand out and waving.

Józef hesitated, looking around. With a deep breath he imitated Kazik's movements, pulling himself up and in.

Once in the attic, Józef opened his eyes wide and looked around. At the edge of the eaves, where the sloping ceiling met the walls, light trickled in from below, casting just enough grey into the space to be able to move without missing the cross planks and falling through. The attic smelled musty, but there was also a strong smell of ammonia. Off to his left, Józef heard a scurrying of tiny, clawed feet.

"Never mind the rats," Kazik seemed to read Józef's thoughts. "As long as you don't piss them off, you're fine." With a chuckle, he began to walk, his path taking him over his apartment and in the direction of the hallway.

"What are we doing?" Józef asked, standing. "What's up here?" He kept his eyes on his feet, making sure to place each step on one of the rafters. Even though the building had seemed empty, he didn't want the sound of his body crashing through the ceiling to the floor below to draw anyone's attention. *Never stand out, never stand out* . . . Not to mention the bones he would surely break.

"People don't realize," Kazik spoke, hopping nimbly over the rafters, "quite a few of these buildings are connected by their attics. If you know where they are, you can go from one building to another and no one's the wiser." He stepped and one of the rafters creaked. "Of course," he stopped, "you have to be careful about *that*. Because anyone would have heard it. And don't fall through."

Józef was amazed, and as he walked, memories of playing spy in the woods as a child flooded him. It would have been so much fun to come up here and hide from each other—and from teachers and parents—all the while pretending that the Enemy was just outside, looking for you and ready to capture you if you made one wrong step. Of course, now, that *was* the case, and knowing that this game of hide-and-seek could end in death, Józef could only clench his teeth and hope.

The two wound their way through the attics for another fifteen minutes, ducking wires, peeling insulation, and rats. Józef tried to maintain his bearings based: they had begun going straight, moving away from the school, and moved parallel to Nicolaus Copernicus Street before turning right. By now, they should be . . .

"We stop here," Kazik said, squatting. "That way," he pointed straight ahead, "is Stanislaw Moniuszko Street, and over there," he moved his hand to ten o'clock.

"Is the *Judenrat*!" Józef said. They had covered almost four blocks!

"Yes," Kazik answered. "But now we have other tasks." While Józef watched, Kazik leaned forward and laid his body across the rafters, stretching his legs out behind him. He turned his head to Józef and lifted his right forefinger to his pursed lips. He turned back to the ceiling paneling, which was six inches under his face. He waited a few seconds, and then made a sucking sound with his lips, imitating a rat. He continued for a minute or so, before squeaking again.

"What are you doing?" Józef whispered.

Kazik turned his head. "Signal," he said, "to someone just below."

Kazik turned back to the ceiling and fell silent. Behind him, Józef held his breath, his heart beating in his ears.

A ceiling tile shifting in place below Kazik broke the silence. Whoever was below had heard the signal, and was pushing up through the ceiling. They'd clearly done this before. Light pushed through around the edges, forming a glowing, wobbling square as the tile was pushed up from an apartment below. It rose slowly, revealing a pair of blue eyes peering up into the attic's darkness. The person must've been standing on a stepstool or something.

"Hello, Sławomir," Kazik said, turning his head and smiling at Józef. "I've brought a comrade."

# FIVE

JÓZEF WAS STUNNED.

When he had lowered himself from the ceiling, he found himself in a darkened room surrounded by piles and piles and piles of weapons, all of which were stacked on rows of wooden crates. Though the daylight was kept out by a drawn blackout shade, the dark metallic barrels of rifles and pistols seemed to glow in the darkness like some sort of deadly spirits. Arranged butt to muzzle, at least two hundred rifles formed a sort of mechanical ladder across the tops of the crates. To their right, three piles of semiautomatic pistols threatened at any moment to tumble to the floor. On the other crates, and spread out across the floor, Józef saw stick grenades, hundreds of boxes of ammunition, bayonets, and several crates of empty bottles. "For making Molotov cocktails," Sławomir said, noticing where Józef was looking. "You see?" he pointed to the corner, where three large, thirty-liter kerosene cans stood sentinel. "We will use these bottles with kerosene—and this is *real* kerosene, mind you, not that fake *ersatz* stuff that citizens are having to use—stuff a rag into them, light the rag, throw, and BOOM! No more Germans! Or if it doesn't kill them, then at least we can have German flambé! Ha!"

Józef glanced over to Kazik, who was shaking his head.

"You'll have to forgive Sławomir," he said. "He likes to joke about anything. Right, Sławomir?"

"That's right!" came the reply. "Which reminds me, how many Germans does it take to run a country?"

"I have no idea," Kazik sighed. "How many?"

"None—go find a dickless Austrian!"

At the punch line, Kazik snorted. But Józef was wringing his hands. He had never taken his eyes off the weapons. When he was growing up, the only gun he'd ever seen up close had been his father's rifle. And he'd never even touched it. Since the Germans invaded, he'd seen guns everywhere—pistols, machine guns, tanks, rifles, grenades—but he'd never been this close to touching a weapon. A weapon that *he* might be asked to use.

"What is all of this, hm?" he stammered, looking back and forth between Kazik and Sławomir. "What the . . . ? Who knows about this? Where did you get these? Do you have any idea what the Germans would do if they found this?"

"Whoa, easy, yellowbelly!" Sławomir held out his hand. "You're gonna make us all scared before long, and that's not what we need right now!"

"Don't worry about it," Kazik said to Sławomir. "It's like this," he said, looking at Józef, "soon after the ghetto was formed, a group of us has been smuggling weapons and supplies in from outside, in case . . . well, let's just say it is not our intent to die like lambs to slaughter."

Sławomir nodded.

"The only way into and out of this room is through the attic. There used to be a door, there," Kazik pointed to a spot on the wall opposite the window. Józef squinted and could make out a two-meter-tall, rectangular silhouette, as if someone had traced a door onto the wall with chalk. "We walled that door up pretty fast, just so we could have this spot."

"Only problem is if someone who knows the building starts running his mouth," Sławomir interrupted, "or if someone outside peeks in." He motioned to the window. "But that shouldn't happen, as long as we keep that pulled." He pointed to the blackout curtain.

"Okay," Józef stammered, "but why are you bringing me into this?"

"Well," Kazik answered, "the Council has been

funneling people our way, and especially now that . . . " His voice tapered off and he looked at Sławomir. Józef felt his heartbeat speed up. He clenched his fists and looked at both men.

"Now that what?" he asked.

"We learned three days ago that the Germans are planning on liquidating the ghetto," Kazik said.

"Doing what?" Józef snapped.

"Everyone is going to be rounded up and sent away. To die. You've noticed that there have been more and more transports already?"

Józef nodded, his eyes darting back and forth between Sławomir and Kazik.

"Well, that's the beginning. They're trying to thin us out before an assault. Everyone will go. Everyone."

"But . . . but how do you know that they are being sent to die, hm?" Józef asked.

"Good question. To be honest, we don't *know* anything. If by *know* you mean that any of us have seen anything with our own eyes. What we *know* is that we've been able to bribe information from some of the guards. If they're lying? Who knows? We've also heard from others on the outside. Others who are in the know. Escaped Jews. Poles."

"Who do you mean by *we*?" Józef asked.

"*We* refers to those of us who have been organizing all of this," he gestured to the weapons. "There's about fifty of us right now. And this is not the only cache we've got. There are three more. We've also been planning and plotting. And gathering information."

"Okay, and then what?" Józef asked.

"If the Germans are planning on liquidating the ghetto, then our time has come to fight. Feliks recommended you to us, and he wants you to be armed and included on our preparations. And if he wants it, we want it."

While Sławomir spoke, Józef's thoughts swirled around Ana, who lay at home sick in bed. They swirled around Ana's mother, who drained herself every day to take care of her only remaining daughter. Around Doctor Grunwolski, who could perhaps offer some form of treatment to help her. Around his work with the children. And around the goose-stepping German afterbirths that had reduced an entire people to the status of animals fighting to survive.

But take up weapons? Kill? Józef felt light-headed. This could not be the best way. The only way. There had to be an alternative. Józef had always been a teacher of literature, reading, and writing. He was not a soldier.

"I'm honored," he finally muttered, scanning the piles of weapons, "but have you thought this through? I mean, *really* thought this through? Have you seen the signs on the walls around the ghetto? Just trying to *communicate* with someone on the Aryan side will get you the death penalty. And did you see the types of things the Germans did to ordinary Poles when they invaded? What do you think they would do to Jews who've been stockpiling weapons . . . weapons to use against the Germans!

You'd be killed on the spot!" Józef was panting, and he was already craning his neck for any sounds coming from outside and elsewhere in the building. What if they had been followed? What if there was someone under them, listening to their conversation? And how could they get that many weapons hidden—and Kazik had mentioned *three* caches—without someone ratting on them? No, it was too risky. There is no way that anyone would be able to keep a secret like that this long—and especially a secret that could cost everyone their lives!

"Look," Sławomir said, "you're not wrong. A little jumpy, maybe," he smiled, "but not wrong. But the facts are these: the Germans want us dead. And either we can die by doing what they want—obeying and going on their transports—or we can do it by doing what *we* want. By showing them that we are *men*! That we are humans!"

Shaking his head while Sławomir spoke, Józef was unmoved. It was insanity. What could fifty Jews with four rooms of weapons possibly do against the overwhelming force of the Third Reich? It was suicide.

"Also," he said, "why would Feliks even want me to work with you? You seem like you know what you're doing. I'm just a teacher. I'm not a soldier! That can't be a good idea. And for you? Wouldn't that be a huge risk, that I might screw something up just when it mattered most?" He was hoping to convince them to leave him out of this. "I've never even held a gun!"

Kazik sucked air through his teeth and scowled.

"Are you serious?" Sławomir asked. "Not even to hunt?"

"No, not even for that! And anyway . . . "

"Okay, okay," Kazik interrupted. "That would certainly be dicey. But right now, even more dicey would be not using every man we've got to fight back. And every man with the chutzpah to stand up to the Germans. Feliks told us you've got balls. And you're not the only one, by the way."

"Only one what?"

"The only one joining us who's never shot a gun. What we need is courage."

Józef looked back and forth between the two men.

"What about hiding?" he asked, looking up.

Kazik and Sławomir shot a glance at each other.

"Hiding?" Kazik said. "The hiding's already started. Have you noticed that the buildings have been getting quiet lately? The word is getting out. For over a year our people have been building and stocking bunkers. Just for this. But what will *you* do? Hide? Or fight? We brought you here because Feliks thinks you'd be better with a gun than with all the women and children underground."

*Bunkers? People in hiding? Already?* Józef looked back and forth between Kazik and Sławomir, his mouth open in disbelief.

"Where are these bunkers? How big are they?"

"There's a dozen or so scattered around the ghetto," Sławomir said. "One's right across the street from the *Umschlagplatz*. You know those doors on the sidewalk that go to the basements? Well, one also leads to a bunker."

As Sławomir spoke, Kazik eyed Józef with suspicion. He was growing irritated at this callow teacher's hesitation.

"Well," he said, cutting off Sławomir, who shot him a look. "What'll it be? It's the eleventh hour, you know, and we can't sit around all day wasting our time."

Józef glanced back into the dark, gaping square hole in the ceiling.

"Thank you," he said, shaking his head. "I am honored that Feliks thought of me, but I can't use guns, weapons, hm. I can't even imagine shooting one—much less at a person. Even a . . . a German." Józef's voice faltered. "Besides, I've got to . . . to do something. Oh, my God." His thoughts churned and he felt nauseous. The sight of all the munitions blurred into a vision of Ana's pale face. "I'm going to hide. I'll figure this out. Or maybe I'll escape.

But right now, I've got to get out of here. But don't worry: your secret is safe with me."

Józef didn't give them time to answer. With trembling hands, he looked up and jumped to the ceiling, hoisting his body into the darkness and out of sight.

# SIX

JÓZEF SAT AT THE FRONT OF THE IMPROVISED CLASSROOM and looked at the nine students who had been able to meet with him that Friday. Since he'd arrived in the ghetto, the number of children had decreased by more than half. Until recently he'd assumed that this was because of illness. But since the transports had begun, he knew otherwise. Since the Nazis had banned schools from the ghetto, it had already been hard enough to try and give lessons while hiding. But now . . . now that the Nazis had other plans, Józef felt that his children were trickling out of the frying pan and into the fire.

Since his meeting with Kazik and Sławomir,

he'd been unable to sleep or sit still. His eyes were dark and brooding, and heavy rings marred his cheeks. His vision went in and out of focus. After he'd left the apartment on Mikolaj Rej Street, he had wanted to go right away to Ana—to warn her and her mother and get them into hiding—maybe into the bunker Sławomir mentioned. Where else? The *Umschlagplatz* was just two blocks from their apartment. But something had kept him from going. It was late, for one thing, and curfew would fall at seven. He also wanted to try and get some rest so he'd be ready to teach the children, who would, he hoped, show up now that the transport had passed. But thanks to his recent encounter, he hadn't slept, and now there the children were, looking up at him as he struggled with his nerves, his jittering, and his thoughts of Ana.

As he looked at his students, Kazik's voice echoed in his ears, "They will kill us all." How could he warn the children? Did their parents know? Which of their parents were still alive? He knew he couldn't tell them outright what he knew. One of them would go home and repeat it, or they would spread it around the ghetto, and people would know Józef was the one who told them. The Council would find out, and he would end up with the Germans. There had to be a better way.

"Boys and girls," he began, "I am happy to see you here, hm. Your health is well?" He looked around the room. Heads bobbed. "That's good. You may be able to see that I am quite tired, you see?" He pointed to his eyes. Some of the children snickered. "But even though I am tired, I want to tell you a story today. Do you want a story?"

"Yes, teacher!" the children shouted out. Their faces beamed and they squirmed on the floor, where they were seated in a semicircle.

"Good. Good. But I must warn you! It is a scary story. A *very* scary story. Do you think that you can listen to a scary story through till the end? And not be too afraid?"

"Yes, teacher!" some of the children clapped their

hands. Józef walked from behind his desk and sat on its edge. He leaned in and spoke with a low, soft voice.

"Well, this is the story of an ogre. A large, scary ogre who roamed the countryside looking for children to devour—to gobble up!" He jumped and spread his arms, his fingers bent into claws. Some of the children clutched each other, tittering.

"The ogre came out at night," Józef continued, "often by the full moon. After a while, it became more and more difficult for him to find children. Where had they all gone? They were no longer in the countryside and the villages for him to gobble down. He would have to look elsewhere.

"Well, soon enough, the forest spirits began to whisper through the trees. At first it sounded like a moaning wind, but if you listened close enough, you could hear the voices speaking. They spoke to the ogre, saying in their mysterious voice, 'The children, they have gone to the ghetto! That is where you should go! That is where you will find them, *ooooooooohhhhhhh!*"

As he spoke, Józef wound through the room, bringing his head close to the children's as he hooted and moaned. The children's eyes grew wide, but they didn't make a sound.

"So!" he shouted, springing to the front of the classroom and facing the class. Several children jumped. "You must know that the ogre is here. Here in the ghetto! And how will you recognize him? How will you know that he is coming for YOU?" He pointed at each child.

"You will know him by his shouts. His banging. His explosions. His knocking at your door and in your streets. So if you hear him. Or maybe, if you hear a whole host of ogres shouting in the street, firing their weapons and shouting—maybe in German, maybe in Yiddish, maybe in Polish—for you to come out, you must hide! Hide in your closets, hide under your beds, hide in the ceilings. YOU

MUST! Because if the ogre cannot find the children, he will vanish. He will vanish away, into his forests."

Józef stepped to the window and turned his back to the class. His throat cramped, and tears stung his eyes. He wiped his eyes with his right hand. The children rustled behind him. He opened his eyes wide and drew several long breaths, filling his lungs to bursting and letting the air go, trying to calm himself.

"Have you seen the ogre?" a child's voice asked behind him. Józef's eyes fell upon two Germans walking down the opposite side of Mikolaj Rej Street and gesticulating at the buildings.

"Yes," Józef said, never taking his eyes off the Germans. "They are green and hideous, with great big, shiny black feet. Almost like devil's hooves."

As the Germans disappeared from view, a shape moving at the other end of the street caught his attention. Someone was running. Toward the school. Józef shifted his gaze to the approaching figure.

It was Kazik. His face was just as pale as yesterday, but veins protruded from his neck and temples from the effort. The grey winter sky shone off his closely shorn head. He reached the sidewalk across the street and looked up. His eyes met Józef's.

"You. Now," he mouthed, exaggerating his mouth's movements while pointing towards the building's entrance.

*What the hell is this?* Józef thought. Images of the weapons cache swirled in his mind's eye, and the rumors about the planned liquidation rang in his ears. Was it beginning? Was it too late to help Ana? Why was Kazik coming to find him here? The two had just met the day before.

"Boys and girls," Józef said, turning back to the class. "Please excuse me. I need to see someone for a few seconds. Tómas," he nodded to a boy in the back of the room. Tómas stood.

"Yes sir?"

"Tómas, I need you to be in charge, hm. You take down the names of anyone who misbehaves while I am out," Józef smiled and wagged his finger. "I shouldn't be more than a minute."

"Ha-ha! Yes, sir!" Tomas clapped his hands and strode to the front of the classroom. He turned and faced the students, planting his fists on his hips. Józef hardly noticed. He was already in the hallway and rushing toward the building's entrance.

"Oh, Józef, I'm glad I found you!" Kazik yanked open the door and stepped into the school's hallway. Józef looked up and down the hall. He shook Kazik's sweaty hand. There was no one around to overhear.

"What is it? Tell me!"

"Grunwolski . . . "

Józef felt the blood drain from his face. His skin became cold and he felt dizzy.

"What is it?"

"He's dead," Kazik answered.

"What? How? When?" Józef had barely uttered the words but he knew the answer. It had to have been after the Germans had kicked him out of the doctor's office.

"They did it yesterday," Kazik continued. "They've been doing searches of people's apartments."

"Yes, I know," Józef said. "I saw some yesterday."

"Well, they apparently were going to let him go when—" Kazik gasped for breath in between coughs that racked his body, worn down from illness and malnutrition.

"When, what?" Józef's voice was strained.

"When they searched him and found a ring. A gold ring. All valuables like that are strictly forbidden in the ghetto. *Verboten*. Everyone knows that."

Józef placed his hand on the wall to steady himself. He felt a weight pushing down on his chest. He was suffocating.

"Oh, my God," he muttered, wiping his forehead. "Oh, my God. My Ana, the ring . . . oh, my God."

"Yes, I know," Kazik continued. "They took the ring *and* the ghetto's last doctor."

The two stood mute, their panting echoing off the bare walls.

"How do you know all this?" Józef asked.

"Grunwolski's neighbor, Maria Fleischbein, heard it through the wall. The Germans were shouting so loud, and she told the Council."

Józef nodded. He knew the Council wanted to know about any arrests, disappearances, deportations, or deaths in the ghetto. He replayed yesterday's scene in his mind and slid to the floor, his hands trembling.

"You see what this means?" Kazik asked.

"This is the end," Józef stammered.

"Yes, it begins. The Germans must think there will be no more need for treating the ill."

## SEVEN

"**O**PEN UP! PANI HACEK! IT'S ME, JÓZEF!"

Józef pounded his fist on the thick wooden door. The knocking and his shouts echoed down the street. Some women at the end of the block clutched each others' arms and stared at him with frowning eyes.

"A shame!" Lizaveta Raskolnikov, one of Ana's neighbors, grumbled. "Making enough racket to wake the dead!" The old woman spat and shook her head. Ever since he'd met the old woman, she'd never had a kind word for him. Only scorn.

Józef ignored her. He had to speak to Ana and her mother. Now. He fought back tears as he knocked. Not only would Ana no longer get treatment, but the Germans were coming to clean them *all* out. He had to protect them—to protect *her*—somehow. What was the world coming to?

"OPEN UP!"

There was some shuffling behind the door, and the latch turned.

"Józef?" Pani Hacek peered out at him, her eyes questioning his panicked face. "What's wrong?"

"Please. Can I come in?"

"Yes," she gestured into the foyer with a quivering hand. Józef stepped in and noticed that the apartment was much colder than the day before when she had been cooking. Inside felt almost as cold as outside. Had the two women been able to eat today?

"Is Ana awake?" Józef's eyes darted up the stairs towards Ana's bedroom. His forehead glistened with a cold sweat.

"No, Józef, I'm afraid she's not. She hasn't woken up all day, in fact."

"Has she gotten worse?"

Pani Hacek wrung her hands. "It's hard to say. She's sleeping, so I don't want to wake her. If only we could get Doctor Grunwolski to examine her."

"Yes," Józef interrupted. "There is something more urgent than that." He paused, gathering his composure. He swallowed twice. There was no need to tell her what he knew, he thought. Even if Grunwolski were alive and could help, that wouldn't make any difference if the Germans planned on liquidating the ghetto. He had no doubt the Krauts would waste no time with someone as sick as Ana. He'd heard the rumors. The old and the sick never lasted long. If they didn't die during the transport, then the Germans wasted no time in—

"What is it?" Pani Hacek interrupted his thoughts.

"Please. Can we sit?" Józef looked behind her at the living room table. She motioned for him to sit opposite her.

"Józef," she took his hands in hers. They were frigid. "You frighten me. What is wrong?"

"You must listen, hm. Carefully. You and Ana must hide. As soon as possible. In the bunkers." He glanced upwards.

"Hide? The bunkers? Why?"

"The Germans are planning on emptying the ghetto. Soon. Perhaps even Monday."

"Emptying the ghetto? What do you mean?"

"Everyone is going to be rounded up and put on trains at the *Umschlagplatz*. They'll be deported. And . . . and killed."

"What? What are you raving? Killed? Impossible!" Pani Hacek stood and began rearranging some books and pens on a small bureau in the corner of the room. She turned her back to him and spoke in a more strained voice. "Józef, I don't know who you've been talking to, but—"

"Please!" He stood, raising his voice. Pani Hacek froze and faced him. Her lower lip seemed to tremor in the gloom of the apartment. "I have it on word from the *Judenrat* itself, the Council! This is no joking matter! There are Jews in the ghetto who are planning to fight back. There are weapons! Rifles, grenades . . . I have seen them! It's beginning!" No sooner had Józef spoken than he regretted mentioning what he'd seen. His face and neck burned. Would she tell anyone? Perhaps ask someone else's opinion, or if they'd heard anything like this? Well, it was too late now. What was said was said.

Pani Hacek sank into her chair and folded her hands in her lap. She avoided Józef's eyes.

"Hide? In the bunker? How would we eat? Sleep? We would freeze."

"The bunkers are stocked," he said, though he didn't know what might be in them, if anything. All he wanted was to get her and Ana out of their apartment and hidden.

"What bunkers?" A frail voice trickled down the stairway. Józef and Pani Hacek jumped. It was Ana. She had pulled herself from her bed and clutched the upstairs banister as a crutch. Her face was colorless and her eyes sunken. This was one of the few times Józef had seen her standing over the past few months. Now that she was not buried in a thick comforter, he could see that she must've lost fifteen kilos.

"Ana!" Józef cried and bounded up the stairs. She greeted him with a faint grin and sad but smiling eyes, holding out her emaciated arm to take his hand. He took her palm in his and supported her other arm with his free hand. Tears stung his eyes. He kissed her on the cheeks, the forehead, the mouth. Her skin was warm but clammy, and warmth filled his body as he held her in his arms. A warmth that he hadn't felt in over a year.

"Józef," she sighed. "How are you? And your students?"

"Fine, fine," he said, leading her back into her bedroom. "Please, let's sit." The two shuffled back to her bedroom with Pani just behind. He felt her upper body waver, but she leaned into his shoulder to steady herself.

"How do you feel?" he asked, leading her to sit on the edge of her bed. Pani Hacek stood in front of the two, wiping the streaming tears from her cheeks.

"Oh, me," Ana waved her hand. "I've been better! I heard you and felt like standing." She chuckled, but the laughter sent her body into convulsive coughing. Józef held her close. Her ribs jerked with the effort. She gasped for breath as fluid gurgled in her throat. Józef glanced up at Pani Hacek, who shot him a worried look as Ana's coughing faded.

"Ana, always looking on the bright side, hm," Józef said, his eyes gleaming.

"So . . . what were you saying?" Ana straightened herself up and looked him in the eye. Józef glanced at Pani, whose strained face seemed to nod for him to go ahead. Taking both of Ana's hands in his, Józef explained to Ana what he knew, ending with his plan for them to hide with others already in the bunkers. Ana's expression went blank and she stared at the floor. When he finished, silence filled the room, broken only by Ana's uneven breathing.

"First the invasion. Then the star. The restrictions. The ghetto. Now this? What else can they do to us?" Her voice tapered.

"Who knows?" Józef answered. "But if you two don't hide, then the worst will happen."

"The worst?" Ana said, turning her eyes to him. "What is that?"

Józef clenched his teeth and looked deep into her black eyes.

"Listen. Ana, I love you. You know that." Ana glanced at her mother, who was holding her hand over her mouth and pacing back and forth. Her face contorted in pain. "You *have* to listen to me. I can help you get settled. Tomorrow. We must do this, hm. You must. It's the only way."

As he spoke, Ana held his right hand in her left, tapping it with her other hand as if to calm a crying child. With a hint of a smile crossing her lips, she kept her eyes on the floor. When she looked up, Józef's voice trailed off.

"Look," she muttered. "If the Germans liquidate the ghetto, there is nothing we can do to stop them. Hiding *would* be a good idea . . . if it would work. But the bunkers? How could the Germans not find them? They'd get us. You know they would. If not the first day, then after. And worse, we'd be in one place. Their job would be easier." She tapped his hand again and lifted her eyes to his. "Józef, we must have faith. Everything will work out. And I need to rest. Here. I'm not ready to play hide-and-seek, just because of some rumors."

Józef dropped her hand and stood. He tried to keep his thoughts in check, reminding himself that Ana had been ill, but . . . but . . . everyone knew what the Germans were capable of.

"Ana," he said, getting on his knees and looking up into her sad eyes. "You *have* to do this. It's your . . . it's *our* best chance to make it through. I'll come with you."

"So sweet," she said, closing her eyes and placing her smooth palm on his unshaven cheek. "But you know me."

"Yes," he said as he stood up. "I know that when your mind's made up . . . " He choked on his words. The tears welled up in his eyes and his throat stung with the pain of all the misery in the ghetto. He looked up at Pani and back at Ana.

And without warning he collapsed at her feet, his body racked with sobs. Pani slid up behind him and laid her hand on his shoulder. Its touch only made him weep harder. He buried his face in Ana's lap, trying to muffle his crying with the cloth of her nightshirt. She stroked his hair, whispering, "Shhhh, it'll be all right, shhhhhh."

Minutes passed, and his weeping began to grow softer. He finally took a deep breath and stood, wiping his eyes and looking down at his bedridden fiancée.

"Well," he said, stepping back from the bed and looking back and forth to Ana and her mother. "It's just not true that we can't do anything against those bastards."

"Józef!" Pani Hacek gasped. "Your tongue!"

But he shot her a dark look. "I'm sorry, Pani, but they *are* bastards—every last one of them. And we're just as much bastards if we do nothing. Ana!" She looked at him with tears in her eyes. "I can't force you to hide. Things will happen soon. But I'll die before I give up on you. I'll die to protect you." He thought of Grunwolski as he spoke. "If the doctors can't help, if you won't hide, I'm going to fight. Can you believe it? Never touched a gun in my life, but I've been invited to join the Underground. And I'm going right now, this afternoon even, to meet with them."

"The Underground?" Pani Hacek looked back and forth between Józef and her daughter. "Is that . . . ?"

"They've been smuggling in weapons. Ready to die for the cause. Or for the ones they love!"

"Oh, my God," Pani muttered, "what are we going to do?"

Józef buttoned his coat and straightened his back.

"I will die before I let anything happen to you. The time has come." He kneeled once more before Ana and took her clammy hand in his. "And know this, Ana," his voice trembled. "If I do die, it will be with your name on my lips."

# EIGHT

OSKAR STAREK STOOD IN FRONT OF THE GROUP OF twenty men crammed into a musty, underground bunker at the corner of Edmund Chojecki Street and Mikolaj Rej Street. Directly across the street from the synagogue. He was flanked by stacks of weapons like the ones Józef saw the day before. Behind him, a makeshift, hand-drawn map of the ghetto's northwestern quadrant was drawn on fading, brown paper whose corners were folding in like scorpions' tails. With the window covered by a blackout screen, a single kerosene lamp cast a pale light onto the room, giving Oskar sharp, almost monstrous features. He reminded Józef of the stories he'd heard as a child of the Golem—a mysterious creature that lurked among the streets of Prague's Jewish Quarter, haunting the minds and spirits of Bohemia's Jews.

Oskar was in his late forties and bore the forehead of someone who'd spent a large part of his life worrying. Worrying about family. About money. About health. And now about the fate of the Jews. Józef knew Oskar from the *Judenrat*; he was the Council's liaison to the Nazis. More than anyone in the ghetto, he knew details about the Nazis' plans that others could only guess. Before the war, he'd been in Poland's army. The Germans captured him only a week after their invasion in 1939.

Józef stood at the back of the room with Kazik on his right and Sławomir on his left. His face was pulled into a tight frown; he tried to push thoughts of Ana from his mind. As he'd walked to the meeting, he'd scanned every street he passed for German guards. He'd tried to visualize what it would be like to hold out a pistol or rifle, aim, and fire. He'd never harmed a human in his life, not even in fights as a boy, and now he was thinking—*seriously* thinking—of killing. He let his terror at Ana's fate turn to anger—anger that he hoped would help him in the fight. With her in danger, his entire reason for living was now in danger. He'd already lost his parents. And now? His fiancée? Before they came to the ghetto, they'd planned to marry in Sioło, where Józef would teach, and Ana would work as a stenographer in the town hall. She'd even already made a good impression on the mayor.

But now . . .

"We're glad you came," Sławomir said, pulling Józef from his thoughts, while Oskar eyed the men from the front of the room. Sławomir sized Józef up and put his hands on his hips. "I see you wore your rucksack and dressed warm. Good. I guess you're ready to grind the Germans into Bratwurst?" Józef didn't answer. Now was not the time for Sławomir and his jokes. Kazik overheard and leaned in.

"*Ach*, you idiot!" he said. "Shut up and listen!"

A few of the other men turned and glanced at Józef and the other two. He recognized some of the faces from different parts of the ghetto. But since he'd moved into his tiny garret, he'd spent most of his time between Ana's and working with the children in hiding. As a rule, Józef kept to himself. He pulled his empty rucksack from his shoulders and placed it on the floor between his feet. He leaned against the room's back wall.

"My friends," Oskar began with a raspy voice. Kazik fell silent and faced forward. "As in Wagner's opera, *The Flying Dutchman*, '*Die Frist ist um.*' Our time is up. I know you have all heard the rumors. That is why you are here. Well, the rumors are true: I have learned that the Germans are planning on entering the ghetto Monday morning for liquidation." A murmur rustled the crowd as the men leaned in to whisper to each other. Józef's face burned.

Oskar raised his hands to quiet the noise. "The Nazis have asked me to provide them with the addresses of every person employed in the ghetto. I imagine that this is meant to be a death list of the higher functionaries and intellectuals whom the Germans will target first. In their mind, it will be easier to control us all if the people they think are the brains of the ghetto are gone. This afternoon, I submitted my list to the *Amt der jüdischen Verwaltung*, the office of Jewish Management, but with false addresses."

Another murmur.

"That should cause some confusion," he continued. "But not as much as what we have to do." He turned to the map and pulled a red marker from his pocket. He dotted the map with arrows and circles.

"From what I have been able to learn," he said, motioning to the top of the map, "is that the Germans will enter the ghetto from the northwest entrance, here." He drew a circle around the ghetto's gates at the northern end of Chopin Boulevard. "I am not sure how big their force will be, but since, in their minds, all they are doing is coming to, shall we say, 'arrest' the ghetto's intellectuals, then we will likely see only foot soldiers. In any case, there has been no organized resistance since the ghetto was formed, so they cannot be expecting anything out of the ordinary." Oskar paused and took a deep breath.

"But we will be stationed in the attics and along the rooftops here, here, here, and here." He drew little stars across the map along Chopin Boulevard, Stanislaw Moniuszko Street, and Nicolaus Copernicus Street. "You will be in groups of three. You know what these are. And you will be armed with rifles, pistols, Molotov cocktails, and, for those of you who will be positioned closest to the ghetto entrance, German stick grenades."

A murmur. Some of the men craned their necks for a better view of the weapons. Józef felt his palms grow clammy at the thought of holding a rifle. Kazik leaned over and said, "It will be you, Sławomir, and me." Józef nodded.

"Those of you with weapons experience will be placed closer to the ghetto entrance. Your job will be to wait until the line of soldiers has fully entered the ghetto. Once the soldiers are in, the gates will likely be closed. At this point you will open fire on the rear of the line."

"Why the rear?" someone asked. "Wouldn't it make more sense to target the front?"

Oskar nodded. "That is a good question. But no: by targeting the rear, this should create surprise and maybe even panic in the soldiers, forcing them to run forward, where the rest of you will be positioned on both sides of the road in ambush."

"What about those of us on the two side streets?" Kazik asked.

"Those spots are to target any soldiers who try to flee."

Another murmur in the crowd. Sławomir leaned over and whispered to Józef, "Hmm, taking pot-shots at Krauts. Sounds good, until they roll in with their tanks and kill us all!" He then stood tall and shouted, "What about reinforcements?" A few men nodded their heads and turned to Oskar to see what his answer would be.

Oskar looked coolly at Sławomir and tightened his lips.

"These will surely come. But not right away. All I can say for now is that those of you who survive the first assault on Monday should regroup in the attics along Mikolaj Kamieniecki Street. There you will receive further instructions. Because we do have something planned, but it is best that I not tell you yet. Let's see how the first round goes.

"A few things," Oskar continued. "We have these weapons, but we have few bullets. Each of you will have ten magazines for your rifles, so two hundred bullets. But for your pistols, there is only one magazine—eight rounds. We got these through great sacrifice. You must not waste ammunition. Fire *only* when you feel that you have a clean shot. No blind volleys."

Oskar paused, withdrew a tiny watch from his pocket, opened it, and glanced down. He looked back up at the men, who were becoming more and more restless.

"It is six forty-three p.m. Curfew is at seven p.m. As of this moment, you are taking your lives in your hands to die like men. The only way we can get these weapons to your spots is for you to take them there this evening—tonight, in defiance of the curfew. I do not need to remind you that if you are caught, you will be shot in accordance with the Germans' punishment for curfew violations. Not to mention that you will be armed."

"Oh, yes!" Sławomir chuckled under his breath, "Let's not forget that!" Józef shot him a look, but Sławomir was smiling and looking down.

Oskar cleared his throat and continued. "And, I might add, we need to be in position now, two days out, because we can't afford bungling at the last minute. Better hold down in your positions and freeze for a day than get caught right when we're ready to take our stand."

There was a murmur among the men in the bunker.

"So, God be with you all," Oskar continued, bringing his hands together in front of his chest, muttering a blessing. The men looked down and mumbled along. When Oskar had finished, there was a rustle as they raised their heads. Józef looked up. Oskar motioned to two men to his left, who stood and stepped over to the stacks of weapons. Both clutched sheets of paper and a pencil that had been sharpened with a knife. One of the men was little more than a boy—he looked to be fifteen or sixteen years old and had a childish face and curly black hair. His eyes smiled and each of his cheeks was dimpled. Despite his time in the ghetto, he looked well fed. His features were rounded and smooth. The other man looked to be in his thirties. He was gaunt and wore a permanent scowl, like someone filled with hatred. His face was unshaven and his lower lip trembled as if irritated by a nervous tick.

When the two had taken their positions, the rest of the men stood and shuffled together against the right side of the room, forming a shapeless line that worked its way up to the boy, who asked each man his name and checked the name off a list on his paper. He nodded to the weapons behind him, and the man leaned over and lifted a rifle and a pistol. The pistol he tucked into his belt, and the rifle he slung over his shoulder. Kazik elbowed Józef to join the line. He nodded and took his spot with the others, his eyes still trained on the distribution at the front of the room. On the left side of the room, the men—now armed with pistols and rifles—were registering their names with the surly man, who was rationing out green metal boxes.

"Name?" the boy looked up at Józef, his hand arched over the paper with his pencil ready. Józef noticed that the boy was left-handed and held the paper at an awkward angle to write.

"Józef Maizner."

The boy scanned the paper and checked off

Józef's name. "Thank you," he said, nodding to the pile.

Józef glanced to Kazik, who was in the line behind him, and widened his eyes as if to say, "Am I really supposed to take this?" But Kazik did not notice. He was chatting with the boy. Józef turned back to the pile, but he had little time to think because the men behind him were pushing in, checking their own names off the list.

There on the floor, a dozen or so rifles nestled butt to muzzle, sleeping. The weapons' dark brown wooden stocks stretched up the lengths of the barrels, which protruded dark blue and gleaming in the orange light. The guns were not new. Some of the stocks were cracked, or the wood's stain was fading. Still, Józef was surprised that they were all the same type of rifle. He'd imagined there would've been a variety because they'd been smuggled into the ghetto. To the left of the rifles, pistol grips stuck out of a wooden crate like tools in a toolbox. Because the pistols were loaded into the box barrel first, Józef could see only the handles—rounded, black, textured grips that ended in a metal ring dangling from the bottom of the handle. The weapons made him feel as though he were in an actual military arsenal. The Underground was far more organized than he had imagined.

Józef leaned over and scanned the rifles for one with few-to-no blemishes. He knew nothing about guns, but he didn't want to risk using one that had even the slightest chance of malfunctioning. He clasped his hand around the middle of one. It was cold and heavy. In one movement, he lifted it and slipped his right arm into the sling. He shifted the rifle onto his back. The barrel struck his head with a thump. He winced and rubbed his head.

"Good one!" Sławomir said from behind Kazik.

Józef clenched his teeth and reached for a pistol with his left hand. He was also surprised at how heavy it was, given its size. Imitating the men in front of him, he worked the barrel into the front of his pants and waddled over to the other man, who looked at him coldly.

"I know you," he said, his eyes empty. "The teacher."

Józef nodded. The man frowned at Józef's weapons.

"Hmpf. Now *you're* the one learning. Take a box!"

Józef leaned over, lifted one of the metal boxes, and slid it into his backpack. Someone smacked his shoulder from behind. He turned and saw Sławomir, who nodded to Józef's rifle.

"C'mere," he said. "Let's sit over there, and I'll show you how to use that. Too bad we can't get you to take some practice shots first, but," he smiled, "that'll come soon enough."

# NINE

**N**IGHT.

Curfew had fallen. According to the signs around the ghetto, anyone caught outside now would be shot on sight—regardless of their reasons for being out. No exceptions.

Józef, Kazik, and Sławomir sat on the ground floor of 24 Mikolaj Rej Street, waiting for their signal. The building's front door was closed. Every few minutes, the darkness was swallowed by the searchlights' circular, blinding white light snaking its way through the streets of the ghetto from the guard towers just two blocks away. Each time it passed, the men covered their eyes to protect their night vision, which they would need to navigate the ghetto's streets in the dark. Kazik and Sławomir held their rifles in front of them, their fingers caressing the smooth wooden stocks. Only Józef kept his rifle slung over his shoulder. Before coming downstairs, he had stowed his pistol in his rucksack, along with the bullets and three Molotov cocktails. Just holding the weapon made him cringe, as if he were holding a dead animal.

Twenty minutes had passed since the last group of three had slunk out into the night to take up their positions along Chopin Boulevard. The first groups had begun leaving two hours before, just after curfew had fallen, and now the streets had grown dark and silent, with no unusual noises, no shouts, no gunfire. It must have been eleven or twelve o'clock. Józef was relieved to see that everything appeared to be going as planned. Despite the frigid winter air, Józef's face was covered in sweat, and his armpits stuck to the inside of his shirt. The veins in his neck throbbed. His ears rang in the silence, and his breath came in short gasps.

*TOC, TOCTOC, TOC.* The steel pipes coursing up the hallway's wall echoed in the dark. Oskar, four flights above, rapped out the signal with a hammer.

Kazik perked up and turned to Józef and Sławomir.

"It's time," he whispered. "Remember: Stick to the walls, three meters apart. No talking! And walk on the balls of your feet. Let's go!"

He inched forward and, steadying his rifle with his left hand, turned the aging brass doorknob with his right. The metal clicked down the empty hall, causing Józef's nerves to shatter with each tinny sound. Kazik pushed the door open and stepped out. Even before Józef could follow him over the threshold, a wall of glacial air met him, making him recoil. He moved forward, and in three steps he was outside.

This was the first time that Józef had ever been outside the ghetto at night. During the day, the streets buzzed with hundreds of people talking, praying, moaning, or begging. Groans, cries, and weeping would mix with the sounds of Germans' shouting or trains hooting in the distance. Doors and windows would open and close. Now, it was as if someone had filled the streets with cotton that absorbed all sound—all but that of Józef's own feet, which thundered against the concrete sidewalk. He trotted after Kazik, whose black silhouette ducked around corners and hugged the wall like a specter. Józef held one hand on his rifle to keep it from bouncing against his now bulging rucksack. He never looked back, so he could only assume that Sławomir was behind him. No noise betrayed his comrade's presence.

The three hurried north along Mikolaj Rej Street, stopping only when they reached its intersection with Nicolaus Copernicus Street, running west-east. Just meters before the intersection, Kazik pulled himself up against the building and motioned to Józef and Sławomir for the two to come closer.

"Okay," he whispered. He pointed westward down Nicolaus Copernicus Street. "The guard tower's that way. At each intersection, we must stop and wait for the searchlight." He held his palm out to the others to wait. Józef's breath came hard and fast. He glanced back at Sławomir, but could not make out his facial features in the dark.

Just then, Sławomir's face began to glow like a light being powered up. Józef jerked his head back toward Kazik and flattened himself against the wall. Like a flaming white ogre looking for victims, the searchlight's circular eye sliced across the façades along Nicolaus Copernicus Street, sweeping back and forth and throwing its blinding, angular light on the street's every nook and cranny. Averting his eyes, Józef saw three rats scurrying behind a body that lay rotting on the cobblestones, filling the street with an eye-watering stench. The glowing eye did not rest. It continued its sweep of the length and depth of the street, until it had moved on southward, its beams pushing their way into the closed shutters of the ghetto, perhaps waking the languishing souls inside.

"Come on!" Kazik hissed once the light was gone. In an instant the three were on the move, now heading westward towards Chopin Boulevard—the street that led straight to the ghetto's main entrance. Where Feliks said the Germans would enter.

When they arrived at the boulevard, Kazik held his hand up once more and the three stopped. Józef saw Kazik's ghostly silhouette ease out from behind the apartment building's wall to get a glimpse of the street. His head swiveled right toward the ghetto entrance, left, and then right again, before jerking back behind the wall. The glowing white eye appeared once more, this time coming from the right. Silently, silently, slowly, it swept the length of Chopin Boulevard before swooping over the rooftops to the east. No sooner had the light moved on than he scurried out into the street and disappeared off to the left, crossing the cobblestones to reach the other side. Józef followed, easing his eyes out beyond the concrete wall.

Off to the right, the grey and black forms of the street and the ghetto's buildings formed a somber, upside-down V-shape as the boulevard stretched the four blocks to the ghetto's massive wooden gate. Józef knew that the gate was topped with coils of barbed wire and that the gate's metal frame was crowned with triangular spikes. On either side of the gate, two five-meter-tall, wooden watchtowers stood. Each peered at the ghetto through its glowing, ever-moving Cyclops eye that hid a venomous machine gun ready to fire at any curfew violators.

Józef held his breath and watched. The two eyes scanned back and forth. Seeing that both were moving away from his location, he bolted into the street, following Kazik, whose silhouette now motioned for Józef from the entrance to a narrow alleyway on the other side of the street. Wrapping his right arm around his rifle to keep it from bouncing, he hurried across Chopin Boulevard and slid into the alley's darkness, again taking his position behind Kazik. In the street, the light slid by. No sooner had all fallen dark again than Sławomir appeared next to them.

"This is us," Kazik whispered, pounding his fist on the concrete foundation of the building behind them. "One of the people who lives here knows about us and should have come down to unlock the front door. All they know is that we're coming. They don't know why."

"They don't know about tomorrow?" Józef asked.

"I doubt it. We're trying to keep it hushed. So people won't panic."

Józef clenched his jaw and looked upward.

"So," Kazik continued, "when the light goes by, we'll have to move fast and quiet! No sound!"

The other two nodded.

And waited.

Soon, the eye passed once again, blinding and then fleeting.

The three moved. This time they rushed forward

together, a meter apart. Pulling themselves against the wall, they slid up to the door, and Kazik reached over and gripped the doorknob.

Which didn't turn.

"What the hell?" Kazik hissed, grabbing the doorknob and trying to turn with both hands. All that answered was a dry rattle.

"Are you sure this is the right place?" Józef asked, his heartbeat gaining momentum.

"Yes, goddammit! He was supposed to open the fucking door!"

"Watch out!" Sławomir reached past Józef, pushing him face first into the wall. He grabbed Kazik's shoulder and pulled him away from the door. "The light!"

At the top of the watchtower on the right of the ghetto gates, the searchlight was creeping in their direction. In the thickening frost of the winter night, the beam glowed and swept across the rooftops, moving closer and closer and closer to where they were.

"Back!" Kazik snapped, pushing Józef toward the alley entrance. But as he pulled his hand away, it became snagged in Józef's rifle sling, and Józef found his upper body pulled forward as his feet stumbled backwards. In a rush of cloth, clanking wood and metal, and grunts, the two men tumbled over each other onto the cobblestones of Chopin Boulevard. In the instant they fell, Józef's arms flailed to regain balance. In doing so his left hand caught the rifle strap and swung the weapon upward. Józef and Kazik collapsed onto the street, and Józef's rifle smacked the cobblestones with an ear-splitting *whack* that echoed down the deserted streets.

In one movement, the two searchlights ceased their endless sweeping of the ghetto and swung towards the men, lighting up a swath of Chopin Boulevard. At the same time, someone in one of the towers cried out in German, but Józef couldn't hear what the man said through the screaming of blood in his ears. For an instant, Józef and Kazik froze, their eyes fixed on the watchtowers. The light had fallen a block short of where they lay. In the next second, they pulled themselves from the ground and shuffled to the alley entrance, where they disappeared. Behind them, the light worked its way down the boulevard, while back at the gates, there was a commotion of Teutonic voices, locks turning, and boots crossing the aging cobblestones.

"They're coming!" Sławomir said. Józef and Kazik penetrated the darkness. From the street, a whistle bounced from the windows and pierced their ears, followed by a raucous shout.

"*STEHEN BLEIBEN!*"

The men didn't stop. Following Kazik's lead, Józef and Sławomir sprinted down the alley, all three holding their rifles in front of them and running. Ahead, Kazik pumped his arms and his legs, the leather soles of his shoes smacking the pavement below, and their dry panting echoing off the alley's walls.

Kazik slid to a stop and dropped to his knees. He reached down to the base of the building. He'd spotted a basement window, which was lower than ground level and set off by a concrete, box-like sill. Now on his stomach, Kazik stretched his right arm to the bottom of the window and grabbed the metal latch, while he rapped at the glass with his other hand. Once. Twice. The sound of his knuckles on the glass reminded Józef of someone pounding on a door—someone impatient to get at whoever was inside.

"Come on, come on," Kazik grunted. Józef looked back toward Chopin Boulevard. Whistles and shouts in German screeched through the night, and the road danced with the small circles of flashlights. The soldiers were approaching.

"Hurry up!" Józef hissed at Kazik, whose shoulder trembled as he hit the window again and again. He braced himself with his left hand against the concrete sill and punched once more. CRASH! Glass tinkled and trickled to the floor inside.

Kazik reached into the hole and with a pop, he twisted the metal latch and rotated the window outward on a pivot anchoring it in its middle. He released an audible sigh and sat up, rotating his feet down and towards the gaping black rectangle, while he placed both hands on the sill and lifted himself a few centimeters. In one movement, he slid from the road through the window, disappearing inside with a rustle of cloth and metal against glass, and a plop. He landed in the darkness below, with Józef and Sławomir following on his heels.

Lifting himself from the dusty concrete floor of the basement, Sławomir sprang back up to the window and slid it closed. After turning the latch, he stepped back into the dark, his feet grinding the broken glass underneath. Kazik grabbed the two from behind by the shoulders.

"Wait," he whispered, squeezing their shoulders.

The three froze, but their bodies pounded in time with their heartbeats. Outside, the sound of boots hitting pavement and cobblestones overpowered the sound of their breathing. Men were shouting in German and blowing alarm whistles. Frantic lights bounced down the alley, casting the shadows of a dozen or so boots upon the closed window, which Józef now saw was frosted. His eyes bore down on the jagged hole at the bottom of the pane, which was much smaller than he had expected—about the size of a boot. He imagined seeing one of the Germans' hands working its way through and opening the window, just as Kazik had done. Opening the window and then coming in after them.

But no hands appeared.

In an instant, the Germans were gone, chasing the men's shadows down the alley and through the labyrinthine ghetto.

"Let's go," Kazik said, pulling the two around. "We have to find the attic." His feet shuffled against the floor as he eased forward.

The building was pitch black. At least outside, there had been the searchlights and the moon to cast some light on the empty streets. Here, nothing but blackness cloaked in blackness, and the sound of Kazik working his way out of the basement and up creaky wooden stairs. Taking a deep breath that filled his chest with stale, moldy air, Józef adjusted his rifle strap and worked his way after Kazik. Up, up, up the three maneuvered—past chairs and doors and what must have been mounds of clothes on the floor. Or bodies. With every step, with every movement, Józef's nerves snapped. Wood creaking. Joints cracking. Breath panting. Goddammit, could they possibly make any more noise?

"What is it? Who is there?" a woman's voice shattered the silence and ripped through Józef's chest and arms. The three arrived on the fourth and last floor. A sliver of orange peeked out of a door that drifted open, revealing a candle and a sickly woman standing in the darkness. Her eyes were large and bulbous, and reminded Józef of a fly's eyes. Squinting, she peered into the darkness, her free hand holding a worn nightshirt over her spindly chest.

"Shh!" Kazik answered, stepping close enough for her eyes to grow wide at the sight of his rifle. "We're Jews—Ghetto Underground! You can help us! We need to get into the attic! To hide—they're after us outside!"

The woman craned her neck to listen. From blocks away, the muffled sound of shouts and whistles trickled over the four.

"The whistles woke me," the woman said, looking at each man in turn. "This way. Quiet!" She stepped aside and opened the door wide, waving her free hand in. Kazik snapped his head around and glanced at Józef and Sławomir. His eyes seemed to say that this was their best chance. He stepped into her apartment.

The woman pushed down a short, narrow hallway, holding her candle like a beacon. As Józef followed, he heard groans and coughs from a closed bedroom. Just beyond the woman, the pale shape of someone's legs twisted from the darkness. But Józef never saw who it was because the woman stopped at the end of the hallway and opened a closet door. Inside, linens were folded and stacked on three wooden shelves that were bolted into the wall. She leaned her head into the closet and pointed to the ceiling.

"There," she said. Józef and Kazik leaned their heads in and saw a half-meter by half-meter square of molding attached to the ceiling. "Push that up, and you're in. Mind the sheets."

"Thank you," Kazik said, lifting his right foot and anchoring it on the first shelf. Climbing on the other two like the rungs of a ladder, he worked his way to the top of the door, leaned in, and pushed against the ceiling. There was a crackle of plaster and a small puff of dust wafted down. Kazik reached down and brushed the dust from the sheets to the floor. "Sorry," he said, and pulled himself into the attic, his feet disappearing as if they were being swallowed by some great beast.

"Bless you all," she whispered, turning to Józef. Her eyes were a deep brown. "I'll tell no one. I promise."

"Thank you," he said, turning and following his comrade up the makeshift ladder.

Once in the attic, the three men worked their way over the rafters like sloths, inching one hand over the next, and one foot after the other. In the darkness, they could only feel their way forward, searching, searching, searching for the solid beams that would support their weight. Push down on the ceiling below, and they would tumble through and land in someone's apartment, the hallway, or the stairwell. As the men moved, a frenzy of clawing and screeching surrounded them. Rats were either fleeing or getting up the courage for a closer sniff or even taste. Józef couldn't tell.

"Now what?" he whispered through the darkness after the three had moved nearly ten meters.

Ahead of him, Kazik froze. "Now we wait," he said.

# TEN

JÓZEF JERKED AWAKE. EVERY BONE IN HIS CHILLED BODY screamed. The rafters had dug into his sides, legs, and back as he slept. He leaned up and swore at himself for dozing off. He had intended to sit guard all night. He could no longer feel his toes, which felt frostbitten in this godforsaken cold.

The white morning light was pushing into the attic through the eaves, which lacked insulation. Kazik and Sławomir sat hunched against the same wall. A fine, hazy slit of light cast a dull glow on their faces. They both clutched their rifles in front of their stomachs and leaned forward, their eyes pressed close to the gap between the attic and outside. They were watching something intently.

The rafter under Józef's rear creaked as he pulled himself to sitting. Kazik jerked his head over, his eyes squinting into the dark.

"Something's happening," he said, motioning Józef over. "Come see."

Steadying himself with his rigid and cracked hands, he crawled toward the wall, clutching his rifle under his stomach. He slid up to the gap in the wall and brought his head level to the others'. The frigid air stung his eyes, which smarted and tingled at the blinding morning light.

It had snowed during the night. The grey ghetto was now covered in white. Fat snowflakes drifted noiselessly to the ground. The streets were empty. *Strange*, Józef thought, even in bad weather there were people wandering around, squatting or lying on the ground, or walking from one place to another. *Something must be keeping them inside.*

From their position, Józef could just make out

the white form of the *Umschlagplatz* a little over a block away to the southeast. On normal days, people avoided this execrable place, because they knew it was for deportations. Only on transport days did it brim and overflow with the terrified, the dying, and the executioners. It was a place of fear.

But now there were people lined up in the middle of the *Umschlagplatz*.

And Józef quickly realized why no one else was out.

In the center of the *Umschlagplatz*, a line of twenty or so men stood on their knees in the snow, their hands locked together behind their heads. Their heads were bowed and they seemed to be eyeing a patch of snow two meters in front of them. Behind them, six German soldiers stood guard, each with his feet planted shoulder-width apart, and each clutching a submachine gun. What looked to be a German officer or Gestapo agent paced in front of the prisoners. Unlike the other Germans, who wore drab, olive-colored uniforms, this man was protected from the elements by a long, black leather overcoat that reached to his knees. His hands were together behind his back, and he was bouncing something shiny in his hands—a pistol. Another dozen or so soldiers stood guard around the perimeter of the *Umschlagplatz*. But they were facing out and towards the rest of the ghetto, and they clutched their rifles in front of their chests, ready to ward off anyone who might come too close.

This was unusual. Józef knew the Germans rarely entered the ghetto like this. The only times he could remember them doing so was either for arrests or to meet with members of the *Judenrat*. But this many soldiers? And these prisoners? Józef thought about what Oskar had said about the Germans' wanting to target the more powerful Jews before moving on to the rest of the population. Was this it? Was the liquidation beginning? Had they gotten their dates wrong? Józef shook his head and clenched his teeth. Why the hell did he agree to this? Here he was: a teacher with a rifle, getting ready to shoot at Nazis.

He tried not to think about how a firefight with these demons could possibly go.

He clutched his rifle tighter, his knuckles cracking around the wooden stock. He glanced over to Kazik, whose eyes had drawn to little slits. He tightened and relaxed his jaw as if chewing something. Looking back outside, Józef lifted his rifle stock to his shoulder. But seeing that neither Kazik nor Sławomir moved, he lowered it. As the scene unfolded, he caressed the freezing trigger with his finger.

"Bastards," Kazik spat, sensing Józef's eyes on him. "Don't you see what's happening?"

Józef turned back to the gap in the wall. The officer was still pacing, but seemed to be saying something to the prisoners.

"What is it?" he asked.

"They spent all night looking for us," Kazik answered. With fire in his eyes, he shot a piercing glance at Józef. "I heard them while *you* . . . slept. But they got it wrong. They were all looking that way." He pointed backwards with his thumb. "And they didn't find us."

"And?" Józef asked, nodding towards the gap. "What's happening, hm? Are they starting the liquidation?"

Kazik shook his head.

"No. The Krauts couldn't find us, so they plucked out those poor fools for an example. As punishment."

Józef steamed with rage. He turned back to his vantage point. By now, the officer had walked behind the prisoners and was working his silvery pistol into a shiny black leather holster on his right hip. With the weapon stowed, he turned around and said something to one of the soldiers, who then handed the officer his own submachine gun. The officer took it and began to toy with the loading mechanism, while the soldiers stepped back and lowered their weapons. The officer turned around and walked to the end of the line.

"Oh, my God," Józef muttered, "is he . . . ?"

The officer stopped about a meter behind the first prisoner, raised the submachine gun, and pointed it at the man's nape. An orange flash burst from the muzzle and the prisoner fell to the ground like a large bag of potatoes. A second later, the thundering report smacked into the men's attic hideout and echoed down the ghetto streets, off the walls, roads, and windows. BAMBAMBAMBAMBAM!

One by one, the officer moved down the line, repeating the process. Most of the men fell like the first one, but a few twitched and writhed in the snow, their crimson blood flooding out from around their heads and necks. When the officer had reached the end of the line, he swung the gun's strap over his shoulder and walked over to the two prisoners who were still moving. In one movement, he pulled his pistol back out from its holster, aimed it one meter over each man's head. BAMBAMBAM! BAMBAMBAM! With each shot, the men jerked once and lay still. As the officer put his pistol away, he leaned over and stomped his boots two or three times in the snow, as if trying to shake something off them.

Józef pulled his eyes away from the window, turned, and sat up, leaning his back against the wall. Sons of bitches. He'd always hated the Germans, and had heard many times of the kinds of things that they were doing to his people, but he'd never seen a murder before. And twenty! At once! He wondered if Dr. Grunwolski had been killed in the same way and if he'd been shot once, twice, three times. Had he died right away like most of these men, or had he thrashed around in agony before the final shot was given?

Józef's face went cold—not from the frigid air, but from terror. Terror of what lay ahead. Panting, he rested his back against the building wall and stared straight ahead, his knees raised and his hands clutching the rifle between his legs with the muzzle pointed upward. The attic's dark brown and black recesses faded in and out of focus.

"Józef," someone hissed from his right. The voice came slow, like a drum beating through cotton.

"Józef!" Kazik snapped. Józef shook his head and turned, but said nothing. "There was nothing we could do," Kazik said, as if reading Józef's thoughts. "If we had fired on them, it would've been suicide."

Józef turned back to the rafters and lowered his head, mumbling, "Suicide . . . today or tomorrow, what difference does it make?"

The day grew and the three men straddled the attic rafters, each of them taking his turn keeping watch outside, while the other two struggled with different positions to keep their legs from falling asleep or going numb from the cold. Each time Kazik sat watch, Sławomir slid up to Józef and continued his lessons on how to use his firearms: loading, unloading, clearing jams, aiming at close range, aiming at a distance, breathing smoothly, and adjusting sights. With his rifle empty, Józef aimed at support beams, scurrying rats, and spots of light around the attic and fired, sending an empty metallic *click* bouncing through the attic. *Click. Clickclick. Click.*

When Sławomir took his place at watch, Józef continued to toy with his rifle and pistol in a flurry of rubbing, scraping, and knocking of metal against metal. The more he worked with his weapons, the more he became comfortable with their weight, their feel, their sights, their shape. More than that, keeping his hands busy kept his mind off Ana and her mother. Why wouldn't they agree to hide? How long would it be before the Germans made it to their apartment and found Ana in her bed? Didn't she know what they would do when they found her? No, he couldn't let himself think of her. Because each time he did, a swelling pain in his throat and an overwhelming flood of memories over-powered him.

Shaking the thoughts from his mind, he bit the

insides of his cheeks and drew blood. With the salty iron taste coating his tongue, he turned back to his rifle and stripped it again and again. Outside, the afternoon stretched on, and the ghetto breathed, sighed, moaned, and cried. When it was Józef's turn to sit watch, he could not pull his eyes from the *Umschlagplatz*. The Germans had left the bodies where they fell. As the snow began once more to fall, they were soon dusted in ice that wouldn't melt. Night finally lowered and the streets emptied. But Józef kept his gaze fixed on the dead, even as their silhouettes faded into black.

# ELEVEN

A FTER HOURS OF SITTING, SHIVERING, AND ACHING through the night, Kazik broke the silence an hour or so before dawn.

"It's time," he whispered. He stood in the dark, arching his back and grimacing as his spine cracked. Sławomir and Józef worked their way up, steadying themselves against the angled ceiling. Blood returned to their legs and feet. Józef winced as needles stabbed at his toes, his heels, his feet, his calves. Three meters to his left, Kazik rustled about in his rucksack, muttering under his breath and fishing for something. With a click, he turned on a small flashlight that threw an eye-splitting yellowish circle on the rafters at his feet. Six or seven large grey rats fled farther into the darkness amid squeaks and scratches, their clawed feet shredding at the wood and tile of the ceiling.

"Watch it!" Józef hissed, covering his eyes with his hands. "The curfew! Lights out!"

"Relax," Kazik answered, turning his back and walking over the rafters, "no windows in the roof. And the Krauts would be looking at the windows, not the roof. Besides, what choice do we have?"

Sławomir chuckled behind him, but Józef didn't turn around. The two followed Kazik, who tiptoed through the attic, tilting his flashlight up and down between the rafters at his feet and the inside of the roof, which was flat at the top. Whenever a board creaked at the men's feet, they froze, listening. From below, a cough, another creak, a rustle. But no voices. From inside the attic, scratches and squeaking. They continued.

"There," Kazik said, and then stopped after they had rounded the crumbling brick column of the building's chimneys. About ten meters straight ahead, the whitish rungs of a wooden ladder emerged from the gloom, stretching from a rafter below to the ceiling, where the ladder was anchored to a plank of wood. The plank formed the hinge-side of a trap door.

"The roof," Kazik said. "Let's go."

The men worked their way over, lifting their feet high and stretching their legs wide. When Kazik reached the ladder, he rotated his body around it so that he was looking at Józef and Sławomir through the rungs.

"Hold this ladder," he said, "who knows how rotted it is?" He placed his flashlight between his teeth and his hands on the sides of the ladder. Józef and Sławomir steadied both sides as Kazik inched up the rungs. *Creak, creak, creak, creaaaaaak.* Once he reached the ceiling, he held onto the ladder with one hand and reached across the trapdoor, where a dark silver, rusting latch held it in place. With a turn and a push, the door opened onto the night. Without another word, Kazik disappeared through the door and into the falling snow. Józef and Sławomir followed.

Morning approached. The morning of the liquidation. The air outside was bitterly cold—even colder than during their cat-and-mouse game the night before. Józef's nose, cheeks, and ears smarted from the sub-zero temperature. But he didn't have time to worry about the cold. Off to the east, the nighttime sky was beginning to lighten into a deep blue. Kazik's cumbersome silhouette had worked its way to the edge of the roof, which was bordered with a masonry lip about thirty centimeters high—just high enough to provide cover for a recumbent man. On the other side, the roof sloped steeply down before opening up into a twenty-meter drop. A fatal fall. Seeing Kazik crouch down onto his stomach and slide up to the lip, Józef followed, his boots scraping across the frosted rooftop. With his foggy breath coming in short bursts, Józef eased his eyes over the edge.

Below, Chopin Boulevard opened up and stretched northward toward the ghetto entrance, its features waxing gray in the crepuscular light. The ghetto's gate remained closed, and the searchlights continued their endless sweep of the streets and rooftops, almost as if the lights were mocking the approaching dawn. Aside from Józef's own breathing, all was silent.

Trying to steady his breath, Józef scanned the street, tracing their frenzied path from the night before. He clutched his rifle to his chest and ran his fingers across the steel trigger guard.

When something caught his eye. Something he hadn't seen before.

About one hundred meters down the boulevard, in the direction of the gates, a pile had appeared on the curb. Józef squinted. There on the eastern side of the street someone had apparently broken curfew during the night to haul out a mound of trash larger than a car. In the gloom, Józef made out the corners of crates, boxes, and chests that had been stacked neatly—almost too neatly for a garbage heap.

"Listen," Kazik whispered, and Józef turned toward him.

"Spread out." Kazik motioned with his hand to the two opposite corners of the rooftop. "I'll stay here in the middle, and you two go to the ends. They're going to come from over there," he said, pointing back towards the gate, "but we are to shoot *only* after the teams closer to the gate have opened fire. Got it?"

Józef nodded. Sławomir clenched his jaw and lowered his chin slightly.

"I don't know how this will go, but save your ammunition. Only take shots when you're sure."

"Got it," Józef said.

"No worries, chief," Sławomir added, spitting over the edge of the roof.

"Good luck to us all," Kazik said.

A paroxysm of fear shot through Józef's chest, arms, and legs. He nodded and stood halfway, his back hunched low, and scraped his feet over to his position. Sławomir withdrew to the opposite corner of the roof.

Józef dropped to his knees and laid his rifle down with a frozen clunk. With numb fingers, he yanked his pack from his back, swung it to his front, and rummaged through its contents, which he had packed two nights before in the bunker. He snatched out five Molotov cocktails, the pistol, a silver cigarette lighter, and three cardboard boxes of ammunition. The roof glowed in the gray morning light, and Józef glanced once more into the depths of his rucksack to make sure that it was empty. With the bombs and the bullets laid out in front of him, he tucked the pistol into the front of his pants and plunged the lighter into his front pocket. He picked up his rifle and leaned back against the lip of the roof.

The morning was quiet. Too quiet. Crouched at the middle of the building, Kazik pulled out his pocket watch and checked the time. He looked at

Józef and held up seven fingers before easing his head upward to look out towards the gates.

*Strange*, Józef thought. Normally the ghetto began to buzz at this time, as people were allowed outside after the night's curfew. Then again, how many people knew what was about to happen? He had told Ana and her mother. How many other members of the Underground had told people they knew? How many of these people had told others? How far into the ghetto's depths had the rumors spread? Were people hiding? Because they were not coming outside.

Maybe Ana and her mother had listened to him after all?

A sound pulled Józef from his thoughts. Something near the gates.

Breathing through his mouth, he eased his head up and looked. In the morning light, the first thing he noticed was the pile of trash on the curb. There was no doubt now. The trash wasn't there the night before, and it seemed a little too well organized. It was as if someone were planning for a move and were arranging their things for a truck to come and cart it all away. Józef scanned the length of Chopin Boulevard, his eyes coming to a rest on the gates. The searchlights now slumbered, black and cold, both turned toward the ground. The guards, however, were still alert: one watching, one gripping a machine gun with one hand and supporting a chain of bullets with the other.

Another sound. An engine revving on the other side of the gates. What time was it? Seven fifteen? Seven thirty? Despite the cold, Józef's hands became slippery, and he struggled to keep the rifle stock from slipping or shaking. A voice. Another revving engine—but a different one. Men talking. Men talking in German. Just on the other side of the gates. Because of the distance, Józef only caught bits and pieces. He could not tell what was being said. But there were several voices. Three? Eight? Ten?

He glanced over to Kazik and Sławomir. Both were lying almost flat, their upper bodies angled upwards so that their eyes would just reach above the roof lip. Both clutched their rifles at their sides, their left hands gripping the stock below the barrel, and their right hands clamped behind the trigger guard.

Another noise. A clank and a scrape. A shout. A whistle. Another.

The gate began to open.

This was it.

The liquidation.

Ignoring Kazik and Sławomir, Józef worked his rifle up and to his shoulder. He knew no one near the gates could hear him, but he jolted at the slightest sound his weapon made when brushing against the roof. Slowly, slowly, slowly he eased the barrel onto the roof lip and guided the muzzle towards the gates. He placed his cheek on the stock, closed his left eye as Sławomir had shown him, and looked down the sights. With his thumb, he disengaged the gun's safety. *Click.*

His finger rested on the trigger.

Two hundred meters beyond the end of the black muzzle, the wide wooden and barbed wire gates to the Aryan side of the town opened. Since entering the ghetto, Józef had only ever seen them closed. He had often wondered what the streets were like on the other side. Were they teaming with smiling *Aryans*, as the Germans called them? Were there children playing? Shops, cafés, and restaurants of all sorts? Was there any suffering at all, unlike that which filled every square meter of the ghetto? But as the gates opened for the first time, Józef forgot all about his previous curiosity. Now, only the black and green forms trickling through the gates and down Chopin Boulevard held his attention.

The SS. The Wehrmacht. Soldiers were coming for them.

The Germans entered the ghetto in two lines—one running along each side of the road. Every soldier held a submachine gun in front of his chest, one hand gripping the stock and the other, the trigger. Their samurai-like green helmets shone in the morning sun, their heads swiveling left and right, searching. No Jews could be seen anywhere. Aside from the Germans, the streets were dead. At the front of the two columns, one soldier walked down the middle of the street. He was pointing to the buildings and shouting something to his comrades. Over the distance and through the cold morning air, a few barking words made their way up to Józef's position.

*"Darin! Alles durchsuchen! Die werden sich wohl versteckt haben!"*

Józef understood a little German, but the only words he made out were *suchen* and *versteckt*—"search" and "hidden."

The head soldier stopped and turned back towards the troops, his arms waving in the air. At least fifty men had entered the ghetto by now, and Józef could see dozens more positioned just outside the gates, ready to come in. The man in charge shouted again, and the soldiers stopped. They spread their legs shoulder-width apart and held their guns at an angle, pointed down and to their left. The soldier lowered his hands, reached into his pocket, and pulled something to his mouth.

A shrill whistle screamed through the dawn, chilling Józef's blood.

The soldiers had already started to scatter. In well-organized teams of four or five, the Germans spread out, jogging up to the doors leading to the different buildings. When they had climbed the concrete steps to the thresholds, the soldiers divided themselves on either side of the door while another stood back, spread his legs, leaned into his rear foot, and launched a violent kick into the door, sending it splaying.

With raucous, Teutonic shouts, the groups poured into the buildings like sand slipping away through an hourglass. No sooner were they inside than more shouts, shots, and screaming bled out into the street. Behind them, more and more Germans oozed into the ghetto like some maleficent disease infecting an already festering wound. More and more shouts, more and more screaming, more and more gunshots. In a few places, Jews trickled out of the buildings, their heads lowered and arms raised as if expecting blows to rain down on them from behind. As soon as they stepped into the filtered grey light, they were snatched by soldiers standing in wait, who pushed the poor souls into the middle of the street.

Back on the roof, Józef's arms and hands trembled, while his eyes stung with tears, blurring his vision. Why weren't the other teams shooting? What were they waiting for? Were they even there? He lifted his cheek from the rifle and squinted towards the rooftops to the north, between his position and the gates. He saw only the snow-powdered silhouettes of chimneys, vents, and rooftop contours. No Underground fighters. No tiny shadows of rifle muzzles. Nothing. Had Oskar lied to them? Were they alone? Józef felt his terror blend with rage. He glanced over to Kazik and Sławomir. Both lay immobile, their faces squarely behind their rifle sights, their hands on their triggers. Waiting. Waiting for what?

Józef turned back toward the scene unfolding below. He froze, a pang of terror gripping his limbs.

A group of Germans was stepping up to Ana's building.

A whirlwind of images swarmed Józef's mind. His finger worked its way back to the trigger. Images of his meeting Ana back in Sioło when they were both students; going on walks with her along the Vistula River in the summers; meeting her parents; asking for her hand; and then her gradual decline as she became ill and more and more bedridden. And now—

*BAM!*

The rifle's stock rammed into Józef's shoulder as he pulled the trigger, and the report rattled his teeth and made his left ear scream with a high-pitched ring. A small cloud of plaster exploded in a cloud of dust from just above the doorframe the Germans were approaching. They ducked and jumped away from the impact point, as if functioning with the same brain.

"What the hell!?" Kazik screamed from Józef's left. "I SAID TO . . . "

His voice was cut off by a volley of explosions—gunshots, thumping impacts of lead slugs into the side of their building, whizzing bullets zipping by overhead, shouts, screams, and more gunfire down in the street. Józef, Kazik, and Sławomir lay flat on the roof and clutched their rifles tight against their chests. With each thud, Józef jumped and twitched, the impact sending chilling reverberations through his body. He squeezed his eyes closed. As the pops and zings and thuds and booms grew louder and more intense, he pulled his arm above his head. Dust and bits of plaster and concrete rained down on his arm and tumbled onto his neck. Both ears rang, and he felt time slow down as if he were swimming through cotton and watching his own death again and again. He screamed, but his voice was imperceptible over the din.

Almost as soon as it had started, the hailstorm stopped. Down in the street, the thundering of gunfire raged and echoed off the buildings' walls and windows. Now it had shifted direction, like a violent storm moving on in its path of fury. Shouts and screams continued to fill the pauses between explosions, and glass crashed against concrete and cobblestones. Józef inched his head up and looked down.

Chopin Boulevard was littered with bodies of German soldiers as well as Jews. One soldier was writhing around, his back arched at an unnatural angle and his hands clawing at the cobblestones as if trying to pull them up to throw them at his attackers. But in one vicious thrash, his body fell still, and an echoing gunshot cuffed Józef's ears a second later. The other groups of the Underground had opened fire.

The soldiers were taken by surprise. In all of his dealings with them, Józef had known the Germans to be well organized and efficient—every movement planned to the millimeter, every order followed, every detail precise. But now the soldiers looked as if some giant had strewn them into the street like unwanted toys. It was utter chaos. Some soldiers ran back towards the gates. Some ducked around corners, into alleys, and behind doors. Others fired back, aiming their shots towards nine or ten different spots along the rooftops and upper-floor windows that spat death back at them. Back at the guard towers, the two machine gunners had opened fire, spraying the buildings' façades with bullets. Their shots fell all over the buildings, however, with no aim and no precision. The gunners must've been panicked.

Józef watched while Kazik and Sławomir returned fire, each taking their time, aiming, and squeezing their triggers. *BAM! BAMBAM!* Józef shouldered his rifle once more and aimed in the direction of Ana's apartment door, which was now deserted. At a few spots along Chopin Boulevard, glowing orange arcs began to sweep from the rooftops to the street below, splatting in a swoosh-ing blossom of flame near groups of soldiers. The Molotov cocktails. Amid the firestorm, the Germans ran back toward the gates, though some had gotten caught by the bombs and tore through the street, screaming like banshees as their bodies burned and belched black smoke into the morning air. When they collapsed lifeless, their bodies conti-nued to burn like grotesque fires placed around the ghetto to burn trash.

When the Germans retreated out of range, Kazik and Sławomir stopped firing and raised themselves up on their knees, growing more confident that they could stand up for a better look. Kazik was mutter-ing something under his breath, his jaw drawn tight. Sławomir seemed to be chuckling as he lifted his left hand up, extended his index finger, and began counting something. Józef, however, was overcome by emotion—not any joy for having driven the Germans back, but fear for Ana. There was no way the Germans would let this attack go unpunished, he thought, and they would be back with reinforcements. He had to find her.

Józef laid his rifle onto the frozen rooftop, placed his hands on the roof lip, and lifted himself up. Before he could come to a complete stand, an iron fist clamped onto his left shoulder and yanked him backward, sending him sprawling onto the roof. Józef winced as his already numb palms scraped across the frost. His elbow screamed at the impact. Stunned, he rolled over onto his back, but no sooner had he turned than Kazik was on top of him.

"You fucking bastard! You *dreck!*" Kazik gripped the front of Józef's vest and pushed him downward into the rooftop. His clenched fists dug into Józef's shoulders. "I KNEW we shouldn't have brought along just anyone! Why did you shoot?! I goddamn told you to wait! This is not some goddamned classroom, do you hear?! This is life and death!" Veins bulged in Kazik's temples and a thin layer of sweat covered his forehead, which caused bits of dust and rubble to stick to his skin. Before Józef could react,

Kazik leaned in and rocketed his right palm across Józef's face in a crushing smack that caused Józef's head to bounce off the roof.

"Get off me!" he answered, reaching up and grabbing Kazik's arms. The former constable held tight, his teeth clenched in a fury. Józef tried to work his legs around to the side so that he could turn his body and tip Kazik off him. As he moved, Kazik sat down even harder on Józef's stomach. Józef felt as if he were going to vomit.

"Did you see what just happened?" Kazik screeched. "Did you see the bodies? That's just the beginning! Do you hear me?! UGH!"

As if struck by magic, Kazik flew off to Józef's right and landed on his side with a thud. Sławomir had scuffed up from his side of the roof and heaved Kazik off. Sławomir now stood tall at Józef's side, his arm jabbing at Kazik. As he spoke, Józef struggled to pull himself up to stand next to Sławomir. Both men's chests were heaving.

"Kazik, what are *you* doing?!" Sławomir said,

his eyes burning with fury. This was the first time Józef had seen his comrade so serious. "We can't fight amongst ourselves, or then what? The enemy's out *there*!" He jabbed his finger toward the ghetto's gates.

Kazik stood and faced Sławomir and Józef. "It is," he answered, "but now's not the time for mistakes! First: there's a plan that we've worked on long before *he* came on board! Second, we don't have enough bullets to be screwing around, shooting walls and getting ourselves killed! We might die in all of this, but I'd rather later than sooner!"

Józef opened his mouth to speak, but Sławomir interrupted him.

"Stop!" he said, holding his hand up and looking around. Kazik panted in front of him, but Józef paused.

"What is it?" Józef asked.

"Do you hear that?"

"Hear what?" Józef picked up his rifle and tried to calm his heavy breathing to listen. But for what?

Beyond the lip of the roof, the sound of crackling fires below trickled skyward. Several blocks away, a muffled shout erupted from a rooftop. Józef turned his head and squinted. Farther up Chopin Boulevard, several silhouettes jumped up and down on the roof. Silhouettes with rifles. Silhouettes shouting for joy.

It was another group from the Underground.

"Look!" Sławomir slid up to the edge of the roof and peeked over. Leaning out, he clutched his rifle close to his side. Józef and Kazik did the same.

Down below, Germans' bodies and the remains of one of the German cars lay scattered about. Yellow and orange flames flickered from the car's hood, and black, acrid smoke formed a thick column winding upward. Aside from the sound of the fires, the fading shouts from the other building, and his own breathing, Józef heard nothing else. No shots. No explosions. No shouts. No Germans.

"They've fled, the fuckers!" Kazik mumbled, his mouth dropping. His eyes darted around the ghetto's skyline and visible streets for any trace of the soldiers.

"We did it," Józef said. Placing his left hand on the edge of the roof, he released his grip on his rifle, which dropped to the rooftop with a metallic and wooden clump. "They've gone." The strength left his legs and he slumped to the ground, his back against the wall. His hands trembled.

"Don't celebrate just yet," Sławomir chuckled, lifting his rifle in front of his chest. "I think I see something still moving over there."

"Where?" Józef looked up. He held his right hand up to protect his eyes from the glaring morning sun. He stood and turned.

"Just beyond the gates."

# TWELVE

A BONE-SHATTERING EXPLOSION BLEW THE BREATH FROM Józef's body. A meter-wide portion of the roof's concrete lip erupted in a storm of dust, splinters, and stinging shards of concrete and pumice. The three men were thrown to their backs. Józef cried out as bits of rock lacerated his face, speckling it with droplets of blood. His ears went numb, ringing from the deafening report. He tucked his head into his arms and crawled away from the impact site and back towards his rucksack, which lay at his earlier position.

The Germans had begun firing again.

But with something much larger.

When Józef got to his bag, he reached out, still on his stomach, and pulled his pack towards himself. His arms and hands trembled violently, but he managed to slip his rucksack's straps over his arms, just as another portion of the wall exploded two meters away from his head. All sound in his ears ceased and the shock wave of the projectile's impact—whatever it had been—made him dry heave. He turned around and looked back at the other two men, who were also on their stomachs. Seeing Józef looking at him, Kazik shouted, but Józef heard only the ringing in his own ears. Kazik pointed towards the middle of the roof, shouted again, and shimmied his way toward the trap door.

They were heading back to the attic.

Over the ringing in his ears, Józef felt in his body, arms, and legs the impact of bullets ramming into the side of the building behind him, and he sensed the air above him swirling in a fury of bullets zipping by. He crawled amid the rubble and moistening frost. New sounds began to return to him: his panting; his throbbing, frenetic heartbeat; his fingernails clawing at the rooftop ice; Kazik's and Sławomir's shouts bouncing back and forth.

Józef was the first to make it to the door, which he threw open with swollen and burning hands. In his panic, he pulled himself headlong over the trap-door's edge and lost his balance. His body and legs fell from the roof and into the darkness.

"AGH!" he shouted. But before he could tumble to the uneven, massive rafters below, he caught himself on the edge with both hands, sending his legs swinging down and onto the rickety wooden ladder with a crack. His face bleeding, he grimaced and grabbed the ladder, sliding down and out of the way of the other two men, who fell down after him.

Inside the gloomy attic, Józef could hear more and more the dull but sharp *THUMP, THUMPTHUMP, THUMP* of bullets slamming into the stucco walls outside. Every few seconds, a bullet succeeded in piercing the wall, sending a lone beam of dusty grey light into the darkness. Those bullets that made it in lodged themselves into the aging beams, sending splinters of wood flying; or they sparked off the brick chimney column in the middle of the building. Józef's gut clenched; he expected any moment to feel the searing pain of a bullet ripping into his body.

"Come on!" Kazik shouted in a muffled voice. Without waiting for a reaction, he hopped over the rafters, working his way towards the door where they first entered the attic two nights before. *THUMP, THUMPTHUMP.* The bullets echoed, ricocheted, and perforated the slanted rooftop. Did the Germans know they were in the attic? Or were they firing blind? To find their way through the darkness, the three men relied on the slivers of light oozing in from the bullet holes and the gap in the eaves, each keeping his eyes riveted on the rafters at his feet. One misstep and they would rip through the ceiling onto the floor below, or worse, the stairwell. There was no time to go fishing for Kazik's flashlight now.

When they turned the corner around the brick column, the men were no longer in the line of fire. But they didn't slow their pace. It was a matter of minutes before the Germans would make it to the building itself. Several meters ahead of Józef, Kazik lowered himself to the rafters, gripping one in each hand, shifting his rifle onto his back and steadying his knees across the planks. He reached down, his hand plunging out of sight as he worked to pry open the trapdoor to the woman's apartment.

He pushed and twisted, switching his hands' positions. He rotated his body to a different side. He pushed again.

"What's going on?" Sławomir asked.

"Holy shit," Kazik said.

"What is it?" Józef asked. His hearing was slowly returning.

"The bitch has locked us out!" he swore and threw three punches at the door. "What the hell?!"

"Goddammit," Sławomir said, "I knew we couldn't trust her! Just letting us in like that!"

"How do you know it was her, hm?" Józef asked. He was thinking of how careful Ana and her mother had always been, always locking up everything just to keep themselves safe. Maybe the women had done the same? "You don't know that she'd do that to us. Or that she'd want to trap us! Why would she do that?"

"Okay, you jackass," Kazik said, "try for yourself!" He stood and gestured towards the door. Józef stepped forward, squatted, and dug his fingernails into the door. It could not have been any more solidly closed had it been one piece of wood. He grunted and pulled, but the door remained secure. The bullets continued to slam into the building behind them. Józef could now also hear other shots, screams, and explosions echoing beyond the building's walls. A heavy firefight rocked the ghetto.

"It is locked," Józef said after trying a few times to open the door. He stood and faced the others. "What are we going to do? We're stuck."

"To hell with that!" Sławomir spat, his eyes

scanning the floor. He seemed to be retracing the outline of the woman's apartment and moving towards where her door was. "I'm not being stuck anywhere!" Holding on to his rifle with his left hand, he planted one foot on a rafter, and with the other, began kicking the ceiling panels. They cracked and groaned with each impact.

"What are you doing?" Józef asked, his eyes wild.

"Getting the hell out of this attic," Sławomir answered. With one powerful kick, his right leg smashed through the ceiling and disappeared as he fell through up to his groin. He was stuck with one leg through the ceiling and the other wrenched in the attic. "Shit!" he winced as he tried to relieve the pressure on his left leg and pound through the ceiling with his right elbow and fist. His left hand still clutched his rifle, which rested across two rafters. Sławomir grunted with each punch.

"Don't just stand there," he said. "Help me! Get me through!"

"Coming!" Józef answered. Stepping forward,

he placed his foot on the ceiling panel behind Sła-womir's back and pushed. The panel creaked once more, and in a rush of twisting and snapping wood, it gave.

"AHHH!" Sławomir shouted, and both men ripped through the ceiling and crashed downward. As he fell, Sławomir released his rifle, which wob-bled on the rafter and tilted over after him. The two men landed in a bone-crushing heap on the hard-wood floor below—Sławomir on his back, and Józef on top. The rifle followed, smacking the planks just to the left of Sławomir's head. BAM! A deafen-ing metallic gunshot ripped through the building's fourth-floor hallway and down the stairwell—the impact of the fall had detonated Sławomir's rifle. He screamed. Józef rolled over and kneeled, wiping blood from his face. He saw that they had landed in the hallway just outside the woman's apartment, whose door was closed. Above, Kazik was dangling his legs through the drooping gash in the ceiling and was lowering himself down, steadying himself with his hands.

"Are you hit?" Józef asked Sławomir, who was still screaming through clenched teeth. Sławomir clawed at his chest with both hands and swiveled his head back and forth in agony. His throat gurgled and rattled. And no sooner had Józef asked the question than he had his answer. The bullet had ripped through the left side of Sławomir's chest, leaving a neat hole just under his armpit. A hole that was flowing with black blood.

"Oh, shit," Kazik said, his feet now rooted on the floor. "Oh, shit, oh shit, oh, shit, my friend." He ran his hand across his unshaven chin, his blood-shot eyes wide and his forehead glistening with dusty sweat. He looked back and forth between Sławomir's face, his chest, Józef, and the building's northern wall, which was still being battered by bullets. Outside, the battle grew louder and more intense. The Germans were closer.

"Go!" Sławomir screeched, reddish spittle

splattering from his mouth. He pounded the back of his head against the floor, which resonated hollowly. Tears streamed from his eyes, forming a narrow, darkened swath through the film of dust. He was panting like a child trying to be strong at the doctor's and not cry, but his lungs were filling with blood and his breaths becoming more and more shallow. "They're coming," he mumbled, sliding his pistol from his belt; he pulled the slide back, chambering a round and cocking the weapon. "I'm done. Done like the dodo," a feeble smile crossed his lips, but his jaw muscles contracted from the pain. "I can hold them off, at least for a little." He tapped his pistol with his other hand and nodded as if to say, *I'm all right. I know what I'm doing. Now go.*

Amid the growing sound of gunfire from outside, Kazik knelt at Sławomir's side and put his hand on his comrade's forehead. His determined eyes bore into Sławomir's.

"We'll keep 'em out," Kazik said, running his hand back and forth like a parent comforting a feverish child. "There's still hope yet." He stood and pulled his rifle to his front. Józef did the same.

"Thank you," Józef said, taking a step back. "Hang in there. We'll be back."

"Go get 'em, boy," Sławomir answered through a grimace. He groaned and tried to sit up, but when he contracted his stomach muscles, he gurgled and fell backwards, panting. His arms fell limp to his side, but he never let go of his pistol, which clattered against the floor. Józef glanced at Kazik, who returned his glance; neither believed what they had just said. At their feet, Sławomir panted a dozen more times, clawed at the floor, shifted his legs, rattled one last time, and let out a final, guttural sigh that filled the hall. Like an angel lying prostrate with two shiny, crimson wings, Sławomir's body relaxed into his own blood. The pistol slid from his hand to the floor.

"Oh, my God," Józef muttered, his hands dropping to his side. He felt his face and neck go cold.

"My friend," Kazik said once more, pushing past

Józef and stepping up to Sławomir's side, where he knelt, placing his hand on his fallen comrade's chest. Józef stood riveted in place, his stinging eyes shifting from Sławomir to Kazik to behind him, where a lull fell in the shooting. A few sporadic gunshots echoed outside, but they sounded farther off, or as if the Germans had shifted their aim.

"Thank you, Sławomir," Józef mumbled under his breath, shaking his head.

At his feet, Kazik clenched his jaw and reached forward, closing Sławomir's eyes, which still stared blankly at the ceiling. Straight at the hole that had dumped him onto the floor and to his death. In the same movement, Kazik lifted Sławomir's pistol from the tacky puddle of blood and worked it into the front of his trousers. Józef glanced around the empty hall and wiped the back of his neck, which had grown clammy, despite the bitter cold.

"We—" Józef began, but his words were cut short as a massive explosion shattered the windows at the end of the hall, throwing both men to the ground. Glass tinkled and crashed to the hardwood floor. White dust rained from the ceiling. Screams rang out from behind the building's closed doors.

"What was that?!" Józef said, pulling himself from the floor.

Kazik shook his head, jumped up, and stepped over Sławomir's body.

"That was no rocket," he said. "That was a bomb. Come on! We've got to move!"

"But Sławomir!" Józef pleaded.

"Leave him! If you want to avenge him, now's the time!"

With that, Kazik turned and dashed back down the stairs *thumpthumpthumpthump*. Józef gripped his rifle tighter and hurtled down after him.

Once on the third floor landing, Kazik spun around and sprinted down the hall, heading for the building's northern side—in the direction of the fighting. Józef bore down behind him, his legs tingling from the pounding of his feet against the floor. They reached the end of the hallway, but a row of closed doors greeted them. Without slowing his pace, Kazik lifted his right foot and planted it into the door, just to the left of the knob. With a nauseating crack, the door flew backwards with such force that it sent the stop flying down with a splintery whack, and the door itself bounced back off the wall and began to swing closed again. Pushing it out of his way with his shoulder, Kazik plunged into the apartment, rifle first, and made a beeline to the windows, all of which had been shattered by the blast, their panes littering the floor in a mosaic of glittering shards. Kazik rushed to the left-hand window and crouched underneath the sill, pulling his backpack to the floor and lifting his three Molotov cocktails out, setting them side by side.

Józef took up position at the right-hand window. He glanced to the right and noticed that a woman's body lay against the wall, as if the person had been trying to hide from the Germans by plunging her head into the corner like a child playing hide-and-go-seek. Unlike Sławomir, Józef saw no blood, and he wondered how she had died. A bullet? The blast from the explosion? Shock? Józef scanned the apartment and noticed that, aside from the body, it was empty. A powerful stench of urine and shit stung his nose and eyes, and the air was thick with disease. But he had little time to think about the other residents. It was time to fight.

Outside, gunshots echoed farther away, but the bullets had stopped pounding into their building. Pulling his pistol from the front of his pants, Józef inched his head upward and looked out for the first time since fleeing the roof.

Chopin Boulevard had become a slaughterhouse. German bodies were everywhere, along with the bodies of a dozen or so Jews. Small fires burned in the streets where the Molotov cocktails had landed. From the rooftops of the buildings to their north, shots rang out as the other teams continued to fire on the Germans who, Józef noticed, had clumped in a few spots nearer their building—in an alley entrance, behind a kiosk, and behind a building's corner. Scanning Chopin Boulevard, Józef realized where the explosion had come from: the neatly organized pile of trash that he had noticed that morning was gone. In its place, a blackened, hundred-pointed burnt star covered the curb and the right half of the cobblestone boulevard. A crater had been carved from the building's façade just to the right, and at least twenty bodies were scattered around the area like gruesome concentric circles. Not all of the bodies were whole.

The trash pile had been an improvised bomb. Made by the Underground and set for the advancing Germans.

"Pssst!" Kazik hissed. Józef, crouching underneath his window, looked over. "Use the cocktails!" he said, pulling out his silver cigarette lighter and flipping it open with a metallic click. He lifted one of the bottles and held the lighter to the tattered cloth protruding from the spout. The orange-and-blue flame sputtered, then lapped up around the rag. Kazik lit two and tossed his lighter over to Józef, who lit three of his cocktails. He lifted one in each hand and looked back to Kazik.

"Now!" Kazik shouted.

Both men jumped up and took a quick bearing on the groups of Germans nearest them. With a *whoosh, whoosh, whooshwhoosh*, they hurled the bottles out of the windows and to the street below. Józef had time to see his first two cocktails splat into an eruption of flame just a meter away from two of the groups, who scattered at the approaching kerosene flames. Kazik's cocktails, however, hit their marks, and at least six soldiers were consumed by flames, their horrified shrieks piercing the air while their comrades shouted and swore in German. Józef then bent down and threw his third bottle, but he did not see it land. For no sooner had the two men begun throwing their bombs than bullets tore through the windows and lodged themselves in the apartment walls. Dust, shrapnel, and splinters filled the room. Józef and Kazik pulled their rifles close and clutched their pistols with trembling hands.

Lying flat on his belly, Józef rotated his body so that he would be closer to the wall, leaving less of himself exposed to flying debris inside. Meanwhile, Kazik slid to the left window and eased himself up and backwards. As the bullets continued to rain in, he tilted his upper body backwards to get an angled view of the street below and to the right. Something caught his eye. Amid the thundering and pounding, he lifted his rifle to his shoulder, aimed outside, and fired. Again. And again. The orange muzzle blast erupted from his rifle like a tiny dragon spitting fire at its enemies, and the gun's report inside the room was ear-shattering. With each shot, Józef cringed, his ears screaming.

"What are you doing?" Kazik shouted between shots. "Fight back!" He fired once more.

Józef rolled to his right and stood away from the window and at an angle so that he could get a view of the outside without exposing himself. He shouldered his rifle and looked out of the window, whose opening was now much narrower because he was standing obliquely from it.

Down in the street, Józef made out a covered green military truck that had rolled in and parked on the eastern side of Chopin Boulevard. Despite the distance, he could see the darkened shape of soldiers' feet moving behind the truck as the men took cover from the resistance fighters' volleys of bullets and Molotov cocktails.

Remembering his dry practice in the attic, Józef slid his finger to the trigger and pulled. The rifle butt kicked into his right shoulder, and his left ear rang with the blast. He pulled the trigger again and again. Each time the orange muzzle blast momentarily blocked his target from view, but he could still make out sparks spurting from the truck and the cobbled street as his bullets struck. What he couldn't see, however, was whether he was hitting any of the Germans.

*Clickclick.* Józef's magazine was empty. Kazik continued to fire. Józef slid back to the window and reloaded, pulling his second magazine from his pack. After that there was only one left. He took his standing position once more and continued to fire.

"Shit!" Kazik swore off to Józef's left. Between shots, Józef looked up and saw Kazik struggling with the action of his rifle, which had jammed. Bullets continued to zip and whizz and smack into the apartment walls, and Kazik yanked at the rifle's cartridge ejector. It wouldn't budge.

"Fuck it!" he said, throwing the weapon to the debris-covered floor and pulling out both pistols—his and Sławomir's. With one in each hand, he stepped closer to the window and extending his arms, firing. His face was twisted in fury, and Józef looked up and recalled something Sławomir had told him two nights before: "Remember to use your pistols only for very close targets. Your chances of hitting something far away are slim." *What is wrong with him?* Józef thought as Kazik fired left and right, left and right, his teeth clenched and his eyes squinted.

"Burn in Hell! BURN IN HELL!" he screamed. But soon both pistols clicked empty and Kazik leaned over to his backpack to fish for more ammunition.

"Kazik!" Józef shouted, stepping back from the window and lowering his rifle. Kazik did not answer or look up. "KAZIK!" His throat stung as he screamed above the popping gunfire.

"WHAT?!" Kazik raised his head, his hands fumbling with the pistols. Veins bulged in his temples, and his forehead was covered in sweat. His eyes were bloodshot and filled with wrath.

Józef didn't hear the shot that did it.

Kazik's head snapped back as if someone had struck him with a club. In the next second, his body had collapsed to the floor, blood seeping from the bullet hole in his left temple. No part of him moved. It was as if Józef were looking at some grotesque still life.

"NOOOOOO!" he screamed, dropping to his hands and knees and letting his rifle rattle to the floor. He crawled over to Kazik's body and grabbed his hand. It was still warm, but limp and heavy. Józef's vision blurred. White spots crowded into the room and around Kazik's body. The bullets continued their unending hailstorm. Pushing himself back towards his window, he felt his stomach cramp. Doubled over on the floor, he coughed, spat, and rolled over onto his back, lifting his rifle over his stomach.

Amid the falling rubble and zipping bullets, Józef lay down on his belly and worked his way back to his window to retrieve his backpack, which lay sprawled open on the floor next to his remaining two Molotov cocktails. He reached out and stuffed them back inside, along with his pistol that he pulled from the front of his pants. Letting go of his rifle, he slid his arms into the straps and lifted the bag over his head. Still on his stomach, he wiggled through the dust and plaster towards the apartment door, which gaped wide into the empty hallway beyond. He reached forward and pulled himself through the doorway and onto the hardwood floor outside. Sliding to his left, he put the wall between himself and the onslaught of bullets, but he didn't dare stand yet. He looked up and focused on the stairwell just meters away. If he could make it to the stairs, he could work his way down and out the backside of the building, away from the Germans and their goddamned guns. Using his elbows, he pulled himself across the floor, the butt of his rifle smacking into the hardwood as he moved.

Two meters left . . .

One meter . . .

At the head of the stairs, Józef rotated his body so that he could slide his way down on his rear, staying low and out of range. Just as his feet touched the stairs, the room behind him erupted in a ball of flame and an iron shock wave that launched Józef down the stairs like a rag doll. His body, boots, pack, and rifle smacked against the wood as he tumbled down, down, down. Pungent, black smoke poured into the hallway from above, coating the ceiling with a toxic cloud. Below, all went black for Józef as he crashed limp onto the third-floor landing.

# THIRTEEN

**W**HEN JÓZEF OPENED HIS EYES, NIGHT HAD FALLEN. THE gunfire had ceased. The only sounds that made it to his ears were that of his own breathing and a fire popping. Outside, everything seemed too quiet.

He looked up the stairs. From the apartment where he and Kazik were fighting, orangeish and yellow light danced on the walls and the ceiling. Thinning wisps of smoke meandered upward from a dying fire.

Kazik . . .

Sławomir . . .

Ana.

Józef sat up, wincing at a pain in his left leg. He

wiped his face, which was covered in cold sweat and crusty specks of blood. He squinted at a searing pain behind his eyes. Gathering his strength, he stood, easing his weight onto his left leg, which was badly bruised midway up his thigh. The blood returned to his feet and legs as they woke up. He leaned over, lifted his rifle from the floor, and checked his ammunition. Five bullets in his rifle, and one more magazine in his backpack. Nine rounds in his pistol. Under thirty shots left.

*Shit.*

As the fire burned itself out upstairs, Józef tried to breathe quietly through his mouth, his head tilted upward to listen. No sounds from outside. But inside? Where was everyone? They had to have had a warning, a rumor, and were in hiding. But where? He'd seen no one in the attic. In bunkers like the one where they had gotten their weapons? Behind the walls? Under furniture? Why weren't they fighting back too?

Shaking his head, he turned and eased his way

down the stairs and to the front door, wincing with each step of his left foot. Sliding up to the entrance, he placed his hand on the brass doorknob, which stung his hand with cold. He paused to listen. Still nothing. He eased the door open and looked outside.

At the end of Chopin Boulevard, the giant white eyes of the searchlights were once more scanning the ghetto with their unblinking gaze. Each time they swept by, the ghostly silhouettes of dozens of twisted, inert bodies threw thick shadows down the length of the boulevard. In places where the Molotov cocktails had landed near wood scattered in the explosion, five or six small fires burned and crackled against the cold. Off to his left, a body smoldered. There were no Germans anywhere. *They must've retreated again*, Józef thought, stepping forward into the night. *Did we really drive them back this time?* Looking up, he noticed the darkness was beginning to fade. Dawn was approaching. He'd been unconscious for all this time.

Covering his nose against the smell of burning

flesh that hung over the street like death, Józef flattened himself against the western building along the street and worked his way to Ana's apartment. He kept his eyes on the searchlights and shuffled along, trying despite his pain to lift his feet.

When he reached the door, it was still open. *At least those bastards never made it this far*, he thought as he stepped into the empty vestibule. Inside, his feet scraped across the floor, sending bone-chilling echoes down the hall. Józef froze, turning his head back toward the door to listen. Nothing.

"Ana?" he hissed into the void. The sound of his voice pierced the hollow silence. "Pani Hacek?" No answer. Without hesitating, Józef pushed forward and strode to their apartment door, which he could find even in the darkness. He pulled his rifle from his shoulder, leaned his ear close to the wood, and tapped at the door with his knuckles.

"Pani? Pani?" he whispered, trying to force his voice through the door without being heard by anyone else. His throat strained from the effort, and he clenched his jaw in terror at each sound. "Ana? It's me. Józef. Open up." He tapped again.

Silence. Not even a rustle.

Józef reached down and gripped the doorknob, but it rattled in place. Locked.

"I'm coming," he muttered to himself, leaning back. With a low groan, he hurled his left shoulder into the door. The wood shook and juddered in its frame, sending a screeching pounding reverberating down the hallway. He pulled back and lunged again, and again, and again, each time his stomach cramping at the thought that one of the soldiers in the guard tower would hear. Or that someone else in the building would cry out and give him away. On his fifth try, he stepped back and ran at the door, turning at the last second and heaving his back into the unforgiving wood. "Argh!" he shouted as a searing pain shot down his spine.

But with a splintering and metallic pop, the door gave and swung inward, throwing him to the floor in a heap.

Józef bounced up and closed the door, whose latch was now shattered. Each time he pushed it to, it swung back in. Anyone entering the building would see that it was open. Holding the door with one hand, he reached backwards with his foot, stretching his body across the span of the dining room, and fished an overturned chair away from the table. He wedged it under the doorknob and stepped back, massaging his shoulder. The door stayed closed.

When Józef turned around, he paused, waiting for the searchlight to pass by outside and throw some light into the apartment—more than the greyish blue that was beginning to tickle the curtains from outside. A few seconds later, the gloom faded up to a passing whiteness, before falling back into darkness. The light moved on.

"What the . . . ?" Józef said when he saw the room. As if an earthquake had shaken the building to its core, everything was upended. Chairs, dishes, clothes, papers, books, bags . . . it seemed that all of

Ana and her mother's meager belongings had been thrown about, smashed, and scattered in a fury. On the floor, bits of crockery lay smashed and in pieces. And in the middle of the dining table, someone had rammed a knife into the wood, leaving the handle sticking out like a sundial.

"Ana?" Józef turned and worked his way to the staircase leading to his fiancée's bedroom. No longer noticing the pain in his leg, he took the steps three at a time, launching himself upward. Even before he reached the top, he could see in the gloom that her door was open. His heart pounded in his throat.

"ANA?" He marched into her room with a clump, and froze. The bed was empty. The room was empty. The apartment was empty. The air was stale. As if no one had moved about for days. But for how long? Where were they?

Standing at the foot of the bed, Józef ran his hand through his hair and swiveled his head left and right. He scanned the darkness. Had her bedroom been ransacked as well? The approaching dawn was still too dark. He didn't dare turn on the room's light because the tower guards would see it. Even though they weren't in a blackout, he wanted to avoid drawing any attention at all.

Then he remembered something.

Laying his rifle on the floor, he ripped his rucksack off and fumbled around in its depths, pulling out Kazik's Zippo lighter and letting the bag tumble to the floor. With a metallic *clinkchink*, he flipped open the cap and turned the flint with his thumb. *Shhhnk. Shhhnk.* Orange sparks spurted from the lighter, splattering the room in a feeble, whitish flash. On the third try, the flame took and the lighter cast a pale, shadowy light across his arm and onto the grey walls. Józef moved his hand to the side, allowing the meager rays to fall on the bed.

Józef froze. Throughout the apartment, everything had been turned upside down, but here—here in Ana's room, the bed was made and clean. As if Ana had never lain in it. Its sheets were pulled tight over the mattress and tucked in around the sides, the pillow fluffed up and positioned at an angle between the sheets and the headboard. Since he moved into the ghetto and visited Ana, this was the first time he'd seen the bed made. Every other time Ana had been in it. Dying.

A gut-wrenching chill spread through his body.

"Józef?" He started at the voice, which came from the darkness behind him. He spun around, fumbling to pull his pistol from his belt with his right hand, while he gripped the lighter with his left. His rifle still lay on the floor.

"Who's there?!" he hissed.

"It's me," came the meek answer. Józef lifted the lighter above his head. In the pale glow, he recognized the withered and worried face of Lizaveta, Ana's aged, nosy neighbor who'd always hectored Józef whenever he visited. But now she held her head lowered like a dog being scolded, and she wrung her wrinkled and bony hands in front of her stomach.

"Lizaveta?"

"Yes. Forgive me, I heard you come in. I knew

you weren't a German. They always scream. You were quiet."

"Lizaveta, what's happened? Where's Ana?"

"How are you alive?" she avoided the question. "Some people thought you were dead."

Józef furrowed his eyebrows. Who thought he was dead? Was she toying with him? Whenever he'd spoken to Lizaveta before, she'd always been harsh and scolding. This was the first time she'd used anything other than rebukes to talk to him.

"Listen," he said, sliding up to her and slipping his pistol back into his belt. He laid his hand on her shoulder. "There's not much time. They'll be back, hm. They have to. You have to tell me where Ana is. Please." He lowered his head below hers, his dark eyes pleading.

Lizaveta avoided his eyes. She tightened her lips as if controlling some overwhelming emotion and shook her head back and forth. She brought her hands to her head and cradled her chin.

"It's been two days since they left," she answered, her eyes moist.

"Left?" Józef stood tall and dropped his hands to his side. His lighter went out, leaving the two standing opposite each other in the shadowy grey light soaking through the window. "Left where? Please, tell me!" He stepped backwards and sat on the bed, his pistol falling onto the mattress. His empty hand gripped the cool bed sheets.

Lizaveta placed her hand on the doorframe to steady herself. She looked up.

"I think they went to one of the bunkers," she muttered, her eyes finding Józef's in the early morning gloom. "That's where everyone has been going, ever since they *knew*." A rush of warmth of hope shot through Józef's body and he stood, his eyes wide. *She listened to me*, he thought, *She did it*. The warmth cooled to frigid despair.

"Bunker? Which one? Where?" Józef ran everything he'd ever heard about the bunkers in his mind, but realized the only location he knew was where Oskar had held the meeting several days before. That was blocks away—far too close to the ghetto gates. He'd heard rumors of other bunkers in the days leading up to the liquidation, but no one seemed to have any idea where they were. Or if they did, they didn't say.

"I'm sorry," Lizaveta said, "I don't know. Pani Hacek didn't say."

Józef's mind swam. His eyes fell to the floor. Images of Sławomir's and Kazik's bodies danced back and forth in front of his eyes. Images that seemed to be mocking him, laughing. A wave of terror and despair flooded over him. His shoulders grew heavier and his legs, weaker. With a muffled *clump*, he slumped to the floor and pulled his hands to his face. His dry sobs echoed through the room.

From the doorway, Lizaveta watched him with tired but pitiful eyes. She shuffled over and put her frail hand on his shoulder. At her touch, Józef tried to yank his shoulder away, as if he'd been burned. His sobs grew.

"Why are you crying?"

Józef buried his face in the mattress, trying to stifle his moans. They slowed. Lizaveta once more put her hand on his shoulder. But this time he didn't recoil. She repeated her question.

"Why? Why are you crying?"

Józef stared straight ahead at the mattress. Where his fiancée had spent most of the past year resting, ailing, trying to convalesce.

"I failed."

"Failed?"

Józef nodded his head.

Lizaveta thought for a moment. "Failed at what?"

"I got two men killed. And I don't even know if Ana's still alive. I didn't try hard enough to get her out of here earlier. I just gave up." Pained gasps punctuated his sentences. He wiped his cheeks with the back of his sleeve.

"Don't you think you're being too hard on yourself?" Lizaveta asked.

Józef shook his head in disbelief and looked up

at the old woman. This was the first kindness she'd ever shown him.

"What do you mean?" He rose slowly and sat on the bed next to her. The mattress gave slightly under their combined weight.

Lizaveta looked deep into Józef's eyes. The growing morning light made them twinkle, as if there were a spark buried deep within her soul.

"You failed nothing," she said in a slightly admonishing tone. She looked at his pistol, which lay on the bed. "You fought back. You made us human again. Isn't that something?"

Józef stared at the floor. He thought. He shook his head.

"But at what cost?" he said. "I'm a teacher. Not a soldier. I'm a failure."

"Nonsense!" she snapped, standing up. Her biting voice pulled Józef from his trance. He looked at her. She stood over him with her hands on her hips. She seemed to have become stronger, more determined.

"For the Jews in the ghetto, you are a hero."

He opened his mouth to protest, but she put her hand over his lips. The warmth of her skin surprised him.

"No," she said. "You are a hero. Never forget it."

She reached up and patted his hand. She looked into his eyes once more, shrugged, and smiled.

"I've had a good life," she said. "Isn't that all we can hope for? As for myself, I have no regrets." She turned and slid her feet across the landing and to the stairs. Her black silhouette bounced down, and the sound of her mumbling floated through the apartment. Through the fading darkness, her voice echoed softly, "Hero, hero, hero."

Frozen in place, Józef stood where she left him, following the soft scuffing of her feet. She eased her way downstairs through the greyness and back out into the main hallway. A few scrapes and slips trickled back to his ears, but soon she was gone.

# FOURTEEN

**S**CREEEEEEEEECH!

The whistle pierced the silence, jolting Józef from his nightmare. How long had he sat there, lost in his thoughts? His heart shot into his throat at the wasted time, and he threw himself onto his side to grab his pistol, which still lay on the mattress behind him. Rolling to the floor, he crawled on all fours around the bed and back to the window, which now glowed with daylight. He peered up from underneath the sill, pulling his head to the right side of the frame so that he could see down Chopin Boulevard. Toward the gates.

What he saw terrified him.

The Germans had entered the ghetto once again, and in far greater numbers. Four columns of soldiers flanked both sides of the streets. Armored cars lumbered down the cobblestone boulevard in a single line, their massive wheels crushing bodies that lay in the way. Behind them, roofless cars rolled in, each with a machine gun mounted in the back seat and a helmeted gunner training his weapon on the rooftops. Another man sat behind him and scanned the top floors with binoculars. If the Underground fighters opened fire again, the Germans would answer with a vicious riposte.

The Germans were walking up to the buildings' doors in groups of four. But this time they didn't enter. Once one of the soldiers had kicked open the door, another lumbered up with a cumbersome, square, dark grey backpack and some sort of rifle in his hands that was connected to the pack by a black hose. At each doorway, the man planted his feet, pointed his rifle into the apartment, and to Józef's horror, a stream of white-hot flame erupted into the entrance, sending massive serpents of black smoke belching from the ground floor windows.

The sadists were burning everyone out.

As the flamethrowers worked their way down the street, Jews trickled out of some of the enflamed buildings, their hands held high and their heads bowed in terror. The moment they stepped into the street, shouting soldiers yanked them from the curb and forced them to line up on their knees, their hands on their heads. Had they been hiding in the bunkers? Józef noticed they came out of only a few buildings—not all. *They must've been all together*, he thought. *But where's Ana?* Józef couldn't pull himself from the window.

Amid the shouts and screams, there was a gunshot. Another. Several of the Jews dropped where they stood. Around them, the Germans swarmed like a cloud of wasps whose nest had just been kicked. Józef could tell that they were frenzied. But he wasn't sure if they were panicked that the Underground might open fire again, or if they were slashing out in their rage. They had been driven back by the very people they'd planned on deporting.

Józef watched as more and more Jews lumbered into the streets. The buildings became engulfed in flames. Aside from their screams, the only other voices he could hear was that of the Germans, who sounded like they were trying to shout the Jews down with their infernal *schneller schneller schneller!* and *alle Juden sofort raus!* and *raus raus raus raus!* Over two hundred prisoners had been rounded up in the center of Chopin Boulevard, their hands over their heads and their bodies quaking against the cold. *BAM! BAM! BAMBAM!* Shots riddled the chaos, and the number of bodies in the street grew.

How would this all end?

Off to the left, something caught Józef's eye. Something moving towards the top of one of the buildings—Grunwolski's building. Pulling himself back behind the curtain so that he wouldn't be seen, Józef squinted his eyes down the street and looked up.

From the first floor to the fourth, tendrils of flame lapped up the building's façade. Thick, black smoke crawled up the wall, billowing upward into the blue sky beyond, forming a large, blurry V. All of the windows were pulled shut, except for one on the top floor. There, a window had been smashed out of its frame, and the gaping hole belched noxious clouds into the air. On the window's sill, a man stood clutching the outside wall with one hand, while his other was hidden somewhere inside— inside the inferno. He seemed to be leaning his head out as far as he could without falling the twenty meters to the concrete below. His head was bent downward. Smoke embraced his back, legs, and head before taking flight. Despite the distance, Józef could see that the man's mouth was open wide. He was gasping for air. Down in the street, some of the Jews had turned their heads upward, and one of the Germans was shouting something, gesturing with his right hand. The German lifted his rifle to his shoulder and aimed up.

The man didn't wait for the shot. Like a marionette whose strings had been cut, he plunged out from the window and straight down. His fall lasted less than two seconds, but his body remained limp the entire time. As if he were already dead. Like a rag doll, he plummeted straight to the concrete sidewalk, where his body slammed and lay still, both legs bent unnaturally backwards. The body didn't bounce. It made no sound. The man just gave up, fell, and died.

All his hope had gone.

With his heart pounding in his ears, Józef turned back towards the scene just below. For the moment, the flamethrowers had paused in their hellish mission. More and more Jews flooded into the street, demanding more and more of the Germans' attention. Józef noticed that the throng of prisoners had begun to inch to the right. The Germans surrounded them, firing their pistols at stragglers and snapping their black leather whips across people's backs and faces. Some prisoners wept, some stumbled along, some glared with hatred at their captors. The Germans were moving them to the *Umschlagplatz.* The soldiers drew in close to the Jews to move them along. Józef glanced up to the rooftops and top-floor windows. Where the hell were the other fighters? Why weren't they shooting? Surely they weren't all dead? He squeezed his pistol's grip and scanned the seemingly empty buildings. Yes, the Germans were better armed this time, but still? Wasn't it a suicide mission anyway? What happened to all that talk about not going down without a fight? Why were they waiting? Józef looked back down to the street.

Then he understood. As the crowd grew and moved, the Germans marched alongside the prisoners—almost too close for guards. The only ones in the open were the machine gunners in the roofless cars. If the Underground opened fire, they would hit their own people.

The Germans were using the Jews as human shields.

Józef's face burned and he felt faint. He turned and looked at the door, and realized it was only a matter of minutes before either Germans entered the building or blasted their goddamned flame-thrower in through the downstairs doors. The image of Lizaveta sitting over her bedridden and dying husband flashed through his mind. What to do? Help them? Hide? Try to escape? He couldn't stay there if he wanted to stay alive.

Leaning over to lift his rifle from the floor, he tucked his pistol back into his belt, stood up, and took one last glance out the window.

Then he saw her.

On the other side of Chopin Boulevard, about two blocks north, a group of a dozen or so Jews were stumbling into the street from the street-level basement door of the building adjacent to the blaze.

The Germans had not yet attacked here with their flamethrower, but several soldiers were milling about in the main doorway. The Jews emerged one by one from the basement. Soldiers shouted and shoved them into the street with the growing mass. There, in the middle of the column of frail prisoners, Józef saw the frame of an older lady holding a younger woman's arm around her neck, supporting her weight as the two women made their way onto the cobblestones. Both were struggling under their collective weight, but the smaller woman seemed on the verge of collapse. With her right hand around the older woman's neck, she held her other hand to her chest as if trying to stifle coughing, or as if she were suffocating in the morning air. Her hair was unkempt and fell in tangled strands around her shoulders and over her face.

It was Ana and Pani Hacek.

They had gone to a bunker after all.

Seeing them, Józef was filled with joy and dread—joy that they were alive and that Ana had finally listened to his earlier pleas, and dread that she and her mother were now surrounded by these vipers. He stepped closer to the window, his hands clutching his rifle tighter to his chest. He jerked his head back towards the open door, looked back outside, and looked at the window once more. What should he do? Try to save them? He would be dead in seconds. Try to hide and hope they survive? No, he reasoned, he didn't know how he could bear not knowing what might happen to Ana. Throw down his guns, join the prisoners, and hope for a better chance for survival together, wherever they might be headed? Maybe the Germans would be more forgiving if they thought he were just another resident of the ghetto, and not a member of the armed uprising. He looked down at his rifle and shifted in place. His breath came faster and faster. Before, all he had to do was follow Kazik, but now, it was just him.

Alone. Exposed. And no escape. He squeezed his rifle tighter and looked up.

By now Ana and her mother had hobbled to the middle of the street and were inching their way in his direction. They followed the crowd toward the *Umschlagplatz*. Józef bit his lip to control his emotion. His eyes followed them, his fury raging at the sight of one tall German soldier several meters behind the two women. As Ana and her mother walked, their faces contorted with the effort, which for Ana was superhuman, even though they were moving at a snail's pace. But behind them, the German knitted his eyebrows and glared down at Ana with increasing anger. He shouted something Józef couldn't make out, but the two women tried to walk faster. The German shouted again, and Ana turned her head and seemed to be saying something. When her body rotated, her arm slipped from behind her mother's neck and Ana tumbled to the ground while Pani grabbed at her daughter in an attempt to stop her fall. This was too much for the German, whose face grew red, and he thrust Pani back in a craze, the veins bulging in his neck and temples.

Ana landed in a heap in the cobblestones.

Beside her, her mother struggled back to her daughter, her eyes riveted on the German, whose hands reached for his belt.

"NOOOOOOOOOO!" Józef screamed full force. His ears rang and his vocal cords seared. He lifted his rifle high above his left shoulder and rocketed its butt at an angle downward towards the window. Just as the Nazi pulled his pistol from his holster, the window shattered, sending a hailstorm of glass shards raining down below on the cobble-stones, where they disintegrated into a million sparkling jewels. Jews in the crowd jerked their heads upwards. A few recognized Józef through the jagged frame of the broken window, but they low-ered their heads and trudged onward. Two dozen soldiers jumped at the sound. In the next instant, their eyes froze on the figure of a lone Polish resistance fighter lifting his rifle to his shoulder and aiming it down the street.

The Nazi's pistol rose. Ana lowered her head, while a weeping Pani cradled her daughter. Just as she had done so many times when Ana was a child.

Józef's finger flew to the trigger.

"*Jüdische Hure!*" the Nazi screamed, disengaging his pistol's safety. Twenty meters away, his green, hulking form came into focus at the end of a contraband Mauser rifle's sights.

"You goddamned Satan!" Józef cried.

*BAM! BAMBAM! BAM!*

The rifle kicked hard into Józef's shoulder as he pulled the trigger once, twice, three, four, five times. The orange, teardrop-shaped muzzle blast covered his field of vision in fire again and again and again, turning the ghetto into a ghastly, screaming image of Hell. He emptied his magazine, and only when his weapon's firing pin clicked into an empty chamber did he throw the rifle to his feet with a crash and yank his pistol from his belt. His ears rang from the

sting of the blasts, his throat burned from screaming, and tears streamed down his face. He stepped
back from the window and lifted his pistol.

When the smoke cleared from the window
frame, he saw that a circle had formed around the
Nazi as the Jews had shrunk back in horror from
the rain of bullets. In the middle of the clearing, the
Nazi's body lay crumpled over onto itself, the arms
bent backwards as if the man were trying to sleep
on bent legs with his torso folded forward over his
knees. The bastard was dead.

But no sooner had Józef realized what he had
done than his eyes scanned two meters to the right,
where Ana and Pani lay in a pile together. Immobile. Their bodies almost glowing the blinding sun.
Under Ana's head, a halo of dark liquid had formed
on the street, trickling outwards and seeping in
between the cobblestones.

His angel was gone. But who did it? Józef or the
German?

*"DA IST EINER DER DA SCHIESST,"* a hoarse

voice screamed back to his right. *"DA OBEN DA OBEN DA DA DA DA!"*

Time slowed.

Rather than duck, Józef swam backwards through the putrid ghetto air, his body slamming onto the ground. The curtains, the windowpane, the remaining glass, and bits of plaster and splinters of wood erupted into his fiancée's bedroom. The pristine bed was blanketed in debris and shrapnel. Bullets ripped through the wall and shredded the white cloth that had covered his love for so long. As death rained into the room, he tried to pull his way back to the door. But his vision was blurred with dust and tears. He gasped for air amid sobs and the bone-crushing impact of hundreds of rounds of searing lead.

He made it to the landing. With the bullets pouring in behind him, he threw himself down the stairs, landing midway and sliding the rest of the way on his rear. *Bumpbumpbumpbumpbump-bump.* The firestorm raged upstairs and outside.

Were those other guns he heard? Some from farther away? His mind stunned, Józef pulled himself from the floor and yanked open the apartment door, which was still wedged shut with the chair. He stumbled into the hall, and no sooner had his feet touched the composite tiles than the forms of five or six German soldiers appeared at the main door, which had been broken open.

*"DA GEHT ER,"* one of the soldiers screamed, his eyes on Józef's. *"ALLE SCHIESSEN!"* Stumbling backward, Józef lifted his pistol and fired, fired, fired, fired, fired, sending tingling pulsations through his hand and up his arm. And piercing, buzzing throbbing in his ears. One of the Germans collapsed while the others leaped behind the doorframe, screaming at each other amid the deafening noise.

Józef turned and ran.

As his feet pounded down the hallway, a volley of German shouts echoed behind him. The soldiers pulled themselves from cover and crossed the threshold into the foyer, screaming as they ran.

"*DADADADADADA!*" someone shouted. Shots screeched through the halls, thudding into the wall just in front of Józef. Reaching the bottom of the stairwell, he reached out with his right hand and grabbed the banister, swinging his body around and up the first four stairs—all in one movement. He bounded up, up, up, his breath wheezing hard and fast in his throat and his eyes dancing with black-and-white spots. Images of his mother, his father, of Ana, of Kazik, of Sławomir, of Grunwolski, of his students—images of so many people who had helped him, or had been kind to him over the years—all reached out to him from the depths of the building, their hands stretched and their mouths beckoning. They were calling to him.

As he climbed up the floors and away from the Germans, his face was pulled back into an expression of agony or weeping—much like a child on the verge of crying, whose mouth shows more of a pained smile than a scowl or frown. If there had been no other noises, you would've heard that his sobs were ringing through the stairway and down the halls—sobs that racked his body and stung his ribs. Sobs that burned his throat and pierced his eyes. Sobs that wrenched the soul of anyone who heard them.

They were the sobs of someone near the end.

When he got to the top floor, he pounded his way down the hallway, his eyes scanning the doors for one that might be open. They were all closed. Closed and mocking. Stomps and thumps and shouts and metallic clicks roared up after him—to the second floor; to the third floor; and then up the last leg of stairs . . .

At the end of the passage, Józef turned and faced the top of the stairwell, his back pushed against the wall and his chest heaving. The window at the other end of the building cast a pale white light into the hallway—one that was almost blinding against the darkness of the inside. The steps grew louder, and the soldiers' grunts now reached Józef's ears.

A head, helmeted and deadly, poked its black form over the edge, followed by the narrow, angular silhouette of a rifle muzzle. Józef extended his arm and fired twice. The Germans ducked.

With one glance around, Józef looked upward and mumbled something to the ceiling. Tears streamed down his face. He looked down at his pistol, whose slide was closed. There was at least one round left. Sławomir called him.

In one movement, he put the still hot and smoking muzzle in his mouth and closed his eyes.

*Click.*

The pistol misfired.

The Germans shouted.

Józef faltered.

The Germans swore.

Józef groaned and looked to Heaven.

The Germans rallied and stood, their weapons gleaming in the dark.

Józef's hand dropped to his side, letting the pistol tumble to the floor with a heavy metallic clunk. The soldiers pounded over the edge of the stairs, shouting and swearing. He let his back slide against the wall and he crumpled to the floor, his eyes wide and his face ashen. His breath came in slow, uneven bursts.

The green uniforms materialized from the top of the stairway like demons rising straight from Hell.

"My God," Józef muttered.

They were upon him.

# GLOSSARY OF GERMAN (G), YIDDISH (Y), AND POLISH (P) TERMS

**Amt der jüdischen Verwaltung** (G): Office of Jewish Administration.

**dreck** (Y): Filth.

**ersatz** (G): Replacement/artificial. Ersatz butter = artificial butter (provided due to the wartime penury).

**fraynd** (Y): Friend.

**Führer** (G): Leader. During World War II, the term used by Germans to refer to Reich Chancellor Adolf Hitler.

**Judenrat** (G): Jewish Council. Group serving as a liaison and administrative body between the Nazis and the Jewish community.

**mensch** (Y): An upstanding, worthy man.

**Pan** (P): Mister.

**Pani** (P): Mrs.

**shul** (Y): School.

**SS** (G): *Schutzstaffel* = Protection Squadron. Branch of the German paramilitary responsible for administering the Holocaust.

**Umschlagplatz** (G): Gathering place for deportations.

**verboten** (G): Forbidden.

**Wehrmacht** (G): German Army.

**Zloty** (P): Polish unit of currency.

In 1943, $1 = approximately 5.2 zlotys.

In 2016, 1 dollar = 3.75 zloty.